Never Summer

Tim Blaine

Harvard Square Editions
New York
2017

Never Summer

ISBN 978-1-941861-35-6
Printed in the United States of America
Published in the United States by
Harvard Square Editions
www.harvardsquareeditions

CHAPTER ONE

IT WAS MID-MORNING when Vlad D'Agostino leaned over the railing along the quarterdeck of the *Magnificent*. He watched as the rest of the crew made their way down the pier and into the city. The sun had yet to burn through a dense fog that lingered, siphoning all warmth from the radiant glow. Rope shrouds stretched upward toward the masts and disappeared into the haze. Vlad raised a hand to rub his eyes. In his other hand he held a rigid object wrapped in a cloth. He stood listening to the city, but soon allowed the unsettled medley to drown in the steady surf that rocked the ship.

Placing the object on the handrail, he felt his heart beat faster, and his fingers trembled as he opened the cloth, exposing the devilish features of a red samurai mask. The captain had once told the crew that the fear of death was an appeal to adventure. The mask did not belong to Vlad, though he had been the last to wear it. He wondered if he might again look longingly at the notion of adventure.

The mask had belonged to a friend. Had it not, it would already have been consigned to the depths of the sea. It now belonged to a ghost. Vlad held it out over the water, slowly loosening his grip. A cool gale sprang up and tugged at the mask. Fumbling to secure it with both hands, he wrapped it back in the cloth and returned to the crew's quarters below deck. He stowed the mask, hoisted his bag onto his shoulder, and made his way onto the pier.

Sights and sounds of drunkenness filled the streets of Manhattan's Sixth Ward, though the wind sweeping in through the masts of the merchant ships that lined South Street smelled of death. An enduring yawn broke against the staggered heights of brick walls, once red, now tarnished by the squalor of the slums. Caught in the crowds of refugees marching between the endless market stands that hemmed in Mulberry Street, Vlad coughed incessantly into the sour air, choking on the lingering smell of decay that had chased his ship across the Atlantic.

He had managed to escape the place where every blade of grass rhymed with the last line of a tragic poem. For him, the narrative of his friend's ruin would forever echo across Japan's Tōkaidō Road. Having fled to Manhattan, he had returned to where he started as though circling back in time. He would have to return to the very beginning if he were to undo all of his afflictions. Knowing the past could not be undone, he needed to find another way to shape his life into something other than an elegy.

His grey eyes peered out from behind his dark, scraggly bangs. Unshaven and unkempt, he anticipated the glances that his restless appearance might attract, but the faces that surfaced quickly succumbed to the undertow that pulled them back into the crowd. They disappeared as erratically as they had emerged. He stayed in the current, a brood of probing eyes, cold-shoulders, and bad teeth, which gnawed at Vlad's confidence of his own presence in that place.

Traffic stalled his pace, and he glanced down an alley, an ominous cave flooded with a bright haze that bounced around a group of children playing with barrels. A canopy of linens draped from clotheslines hung low over the passage of worn stones, a sloppy mural damp and soiled with the cheap liquor that spilled over the lower east side of Manhattan.

As the children disappeared into the luminous obscurity of sunlight and linens, an old man walked out onto a balcony near the mouth of the alley and froze, fixed in an empty gaze. Vlad noted the man's stillness in contrast with the encumbered throng forcing its way down the street.

Stepping around a group of meanderers, he caught a glimpse of several determined-looking men strutting purposefully and eyeing each person they passed. The sight stole the air from his lungs. His heart pounded in his chest, and his skin grew hot as the men drew closer.

From up on the balcony indifferent eyes looked down, unmoved by the advancing episode.

He gazed too long at the indifferent eyes above. The tallest of the antagonizing men, who approached on the street, threw his shoulder into Vlad's as they passed one another. The blow spun him around, and he locked eyes with the tall man, who had stopped walking. He needed to exist, but the man's glare appeared to argue against him. Vlad lowered his head, and turned to continue on without looking back. He focused painfully on the fermenting ground, as though one of the callous stones had recoiled against his chest.

His appearance was a provocation; he was sure of it. The English gangs disliked anyone who didn't look, talk, or pray like them. At least his deep-landing eyes and aggressive features were enough to ensure he would not be mistaken for an Irishman. An Irishman would not have been let off so easily. He wondered if he would exchange the burden of not knowing his roots for the burden of being Irish in New York.

He would be the first to admit that D'Agostino was an unusual name for someone named Vlad. The Daughters of Charity were surely responsible, but he wasn't going to go back to St. Louis to ask them. He promised himself he would never again set foot in Mullanphy Hospital.

Looking up, he peered into the recess between two buildings. The narrow alley ended abruptly with three boys huddled against a wall, swaddled in filth, their bare feet warmed by the foul air that rose from a steel grate. Pushing onward, trying to outstep the smell, he pulled a handkerchief from his coat and coughed bright red into the open cloth. After wiping his mouth with the handkerchief, he stuffed it back into his pocket, appalled at the confession he had coughed up against his will. Admitting death as a miserable certainty was only necessary if one were to grant it any thought.

Atop a building on the other side of the street, a naked boy stood silhouetted against the white glow that continued to bear down on the neighborhood. Below the boy, lofty iron balconies littered the brick facade of what Vlad discerned as a boarding house.

Inside, a long bench separated the clerk from the lobby. On the floor, beneath a window that muffled the perpetual hum of the street, a man wearing only one shoe lay limp, curled up in the corner. Vlad's mouth was dry and he was beginning to perspire as he watched the man's bare foot, looking for any sign of movement. He assured himself the man was sleeping, though he appeared as no more than a corpse.

"Can I help you?" asked the clerk.

"How much for a room?" asked Vlad, still looking at the man with one shoe.

"Seven cents a bunk," replied the clerk.

"No," said Vlad, looking up at the ceiling. "I want a room. One with a balcony."

The clerk eyed Vlad for a moment, until his concern was understood, and Vlad removed a roll of cash from his coat. Upon seeing the cash, the clerk bent over and began rummaging through a drawer. He stood holding two keys, and after staring intently at one of them, he set it on the bench and tossed the other back in the drawer.

Upstairs, Vlad had to play with the key to open the door. The tenement was dilapidated and small, but clean. There was room for little more than the bed, a loose frame with missing spindles and slats that outstretched the mattress. A metal bucket sat atop a wooden stool beside the bed. Cracks in the plaster above the bed struck him as wounds, revealing narrow boards aligned like ribs within the wall. He set his bag on the floor by the bed, and pulled a wooden chair away from the door that led to the balcony.

He stepped through the door with the conviction of a sinking swimmer resurfacing for air, the first breath drawn from the same sky that might have hung over a thousand pleasant memories, or a thousand others. The fog over the shantytown had finally lifted, but the angle of indifference that he had hoped to find on his balcony opened up senselessly to a pale sky that watched in apathy, while he and a thousand memories drowned in the elixir of the slums. Whatever had inspired stillness for the old man with the empty gaze, it was not the balcony. Perhaps it was old age, but that was something he did not have time for. He began to wish he had pushed on in search of a more agreeable tenement.

Looking down the street, he could see the opening of the narrow alley where three boys had been left to rot in their filth. The smell came back to him. He felt his head spinning as he tried to push the smell from his mind, but he couldn't separate it from the cool air choking his lungs. He pulled out his handkerchief and stumbled into the door. He didn't remember closing it. His vision was failing as he fumbled for the doorknob. The bed was his only refuge, but he could not reach it, for the door from the balcony led only to another door, and after that another. It was a scene from a bad dream, over and over. By the time he managed the third door, it was too late to turn back, for all light had faded from his view. Racing his heart, he stumbled forward, reaching for the inevitable door that stood closed before him, but nothing remained. Falling deep into the darkness, the heavy weight of his consciousness outstripped him.

CHAPTER TWO

EVENING FOUND VLAD gasping for air and coughing out foul memories. Rolling his head on his pillow, he peered down a row of lifeless bodies tucked beneath drab blankets soiled with infirmity. The beds lay still like a row of graves, the next line of advance on the frontier of a world slowly dying from consumption. A dark figure approached slowly from behind, like a giant spider preparing to feed on the bodies cocooned in their blankets. He fought an impulse to cry out for help, as it would draw attention from the spider.

A candle was lit against the last light that brushed against the window, and he realized he was in his room. The row of bodies trapped in their blankets had been the sleepy-eyed apprehension of his coat lying on the table, and the shadowy spider was a man holding a stethoscope.

A young woman took a seat in the wooden chair by the balcony door and hid behind a canvas clamped to an easel. The scene lent a confusing impression, and left Vlad fumbling to tether a vague emotion to the loose strands of his imagination. He wondered if he was still dreaming. He sat up in his bed, wondering if he had managed to faint in it, or if the man with the stethoscope had placed him there. Recalling his retreat through the doors, he feared he must have collapsed outside his room, and possibly inside someone else's.

"Hello," said the woman, peeking around the easel.

She was real. In the low light, he could not decide on the color of her hair, though he was overcome by an attraction to her large eyes and the white of her smile.

"Are you feeling better?" she asked.

The man with the stethoscope sat down on the stool next to the bed. The lenses of his spectacles were unusually small, causing them to appear as though they belonged to a child. He wore them on the tip of his nose, and the length of the arms stretching around his head gave the effect of an odd necklace hanging from his ears. A break in his hairline rose high onto his head, an inlet of sorts like a small bay along a shoreline, exposing skin that Vlad assumed to be a scar. He fixed the stethoscope in his ears and held up the chestpiece as if to say, 'May I?'

Vlad moved his arms to his sides, exposing himself to the cool air and the frigid metal of the stethoscope's chestpiece, which he could feel through his shirt.

"This is Edwin," said the woman. "He's an intern at the public dispensary. I asked him to come, after you stumbled into my room."

"I'm terribly sorry," said Vlad. "I don't remember–"

As Vlad spoke, Edwin sat up abruptly, lifting the chestpiece. He closed his eyes, and exhaled deeply through his nose.

"Sorry," said Vlad.

"Just try to remain silent and breathe normally," said Edwin.

Vlad looked to the artist, whom he could see smiling behind her canvas. Their eyes met, and Vlad's smile prompted Edwin to look over his shoulder at the artist, who quickly turned back to her canvas with an air of seriousness. Vlad continued to watch her, intrigued by the mystery of the easel. He found himself wanting to know her name, and was about to ask, when he remembered Edwin, who had since resumed his work with the chestpiece, repositioning it at various points over Vlad's shirt as he listened.

"I hope you don't mind," said the artist, and turned the canvas to Vlad.

Observing the canvas, he made out the pale face of a young man whom he might have considered handsome were it not for his familiarity. It was partly his humility, and partly the same careful scrutiny with which most judge their own faces, that bade him not to consider it too fondly.

The pale face stood out on the canvas in contrast to the darker details obscured by the low light of the room. His likeness lay cocooned in bed, and as he looked at the picture, he admitted the possibility that the figure might emerge from the covers transformed, but conceded to the likelihood that this subject had been laid to rest, or bound up as food for spiders. Pale was not a fair description. In contrast with his black hair, the face was ghostly white. The eyes were shut and, admittedly, there was something he liked in the features of that face.

"Is that me?" he asked.

Edwin sat up, and Vlad watched as he removed the earpieces of the stethoscope. "It's not good," said Edwin, attaching the words to the end of a sigh.

"Have I done you justice?" said the artist.

He looked back to the painting, and Edwin turned to look with him.

"Did I really look so peaceful?" he asked.

The artist leaned around to view the canvas and tilted her head as she observed. In that light he could see her hair was red. "Is he peaceful," the artist pondered aloud, "or simply exhausted from possession? It is said that those with the Romantic Disease become poetic as the body is relinquished to consumption. Inspiration is so eager to emerge that it burns up the body from within." She paused to find Vlad's gaze. "Are you a poet?"

Vlad was silent for a time. In spite of his efforts to reconcile a particular disposition, he always felt things more deeply than he understood them. Perhaps it was a propensity ripe for poetic inspiration, and all he needed was the words. At present, it was a sense of irony that he felt. "I'm told that my mother died of consumption," he said at last. "I never knew her. I suppose it is likely that all I shall ever know of her is the misfortune of this disease that we have shared. That's rather poetic, don't you think?"

"It's true," remarked the artist, smiling. "You are a poet."

"What is your name?" he asked.

"Molly," was her answer. "What is yours?"

"Vlad," he told her, then turned to Edwin. "How long do I have?"

"It's hard to say," said Edwin, peering over his spectacles. "Weeks, months, but not years. Your lungs do not have years."

Vlad looked at his hands as he placed them back on his chest. He'd suspected as much, though he had no desire to consult a physician for confirmation. The better part of his life had served to confirm his expectation that faith in good health was enough to maintain it. This was in contrast with his belief that the phenomenon ran in reverse for everything else. Until that moment, he had never been reluctant to work through an anomaly. Still looking at his hands, he realized he was lying as one would be laid to rest in a coffin.

"You have painted me on my deathbed?" said Vlad, addressing Molly.

"Your countenance is the envy of all higher society," returned Molly.

"That's ridiculous," he said. "You are very talented, but I have looked long enough at this ghost of myself." He said this mostly out of modesty, though it was his habit to avoid acknowledging any evidence of his disease. Still, he wanted to remember the peaceful demeanor he had observed in the portrait. To earn such a countenance was a worthy goal.

Edwin stood, gathering his things, and Molly turned the canvas back to herself. It was true, Vlad believed her remark about the appeal in his appearance was ridiculous, but it left him pondering over the implications. Perhaps he and Molly shared an attraction.

"There is a physician by the name of Gordon Newhall," said Edwin. "He may be able to help you, if you could make it to him. He left in the spring for the mountains out west, to find a suitable place for his infirmary. He meant to take advantage of provisions fostered by the Pike's Peak Gold Rush. His prognosis for consumption is centered on the alpine air."

"You are uncertain of his whereabouts?" questioned Vlad.

"He said the Indians called the place 'Never Summer'," answered Edwin. "That is where he was headed."

Vlad lay quiet, trying to imagine the alpine peaks of a place called Never Summer, and contemplated the possibility of finding this physician.

"Molly," Edwin called to her with a questioning tone.

"Go ahead, Edwin," she said. "I'm going to touch up this background a bit. Thank you for coming."

"Thank you," Vlad said to Edwin, though he was preoccupied with the idea of being alone with Molly. He wondered if she was truly that devoted to the nuances of her painting, or if some other interest compelled her to stay in his room.

Edwin returned a nod and opened the door. Vlad watched as he shut himself out into the dark hallway. A surreal emotion returned, and, again, he felt as though he were dreaming. Perhaps he had died, and his consciousness merely hung on this concluding memory of his room, the last flicker of the candle flame before the wax begins to cool. The room was all that was left. Edwin had faded into the dark void beyond the door, and Vlad did not want to lose Molly to the same fate. He did not want to be left alone with the painting, alone with himself.

"It's an interesting necklace that you wear," said Molly, looking up from the painting.

"It belonged to my mother," said Vlad, running his fingers over his shirt to find it, and wondering at the liberties Molly had taken while he was unconscious.

"I've seen that engraving before," said Molly.

Vlad pushed his head higher onto his pillow. "I haven't," he said. "Where have you seen it? Do you know what it means?"

"No," she said, "but I have seen it engraved on a revolver."

"Where?" he asked.

"In a house on Washington Square," answered Molly. "The owner keeps it in a glass-topped case in his study."

"Do you know him?" pressed Vlad.

"Yes," said Molly. "I work for him on Sundays, so that his housemaid can have the day off. His name is Allen Robertson, and he is a philandering wretch." She paused as though waiting for Vlad to comment, then looked back to her painting and continued: "I see the revolver when I'm dusting the windowsills in the study. I've heard Mr. Robertson bragging about how he practically stole it from a poor Irishman who had no choice but to accept his offer."

"Why do you work for someone whom you hold in such poor regard?" asked Vlad.

"It pays better than sewing," said Molly, "and working one day a week gives me time to focus on my painting. I am slowly acquiring a fair amount of sitters. Perhaps, I will quit Mr. Robertson." After a pause, she glanced up at Vlad. "You are the best sitter I've painted," she said, smiling.

"I was unconscious," said Vlad, "and nearly a corpse."

"Oh," said Molly, "Edwin doesn't know everything. He is still only an intern." She stood and placed her brush on the easel. "Are you going to go out west to find that doctor?"

"I suppose I will," he answered.

"Would you like me to stay?" she asked.

"If you like," answered Vlad, choosing his words to mask his excitement.

Molly began to undress, sliding her clothes onto the floor. Vlad's eyes widened in astonishment. He rolled onto his side to watch her, drawn again to the white of her teeth, surprised to find a bashful smile. When she had finished, she jumped quickly into the bed. The candle flame provided only the sentiment of warmth, and it flickered at the cold touch of darkness that reached in around the window frame.

Under the covers Molly pressed herself into Vlad and tugged at the bottom of his shirt. "I'll bet you've never met a female painter before," she said, smiling.

"I should like to meet more," said Vlad.

Molly nudged his lips with hers, and he kissed her until he felt he would suffocate in the intensity. Catching his breath, he began again in an imploring repetition, a litany of penniless prayer, until at last his clothes lay atop hers on the floor, and eager shadows overran the last flicker of the candle. Fading into the dead of night, the disheveled room slept upon the incurable dream of resurrection in the light of a new day.

CHAPTER THREE

THE SOFT GLOW OF DAWN snuck into the tenement, exposing the cold half of the mattress where Molly had slept. A chill pushed Vlad's heart toward the floor where his clothes lay scattered and alone. His thoughts spun in a whirlwind of incomplete notions. He stared blankly at the floor while he concentrated on stopping the stream of consciousness that swept him through recent dreams and memories. He struggled against the current, pilfering through the acuities that drifted by, trying to piece them into some coherent form. If he could string the pieces together, a complete picture might inspire him to get out of bed.

From the corner of his eye, he caught a glimpse of lines leaning askew into a shy glimmer from the window. He sat up and brought the easel into a clear focus. The canvas was gone, no portrait of a dying man, no brush strokes as evidence of a painter's hand, but the easel was enough. Of course, the canvas had to be removed to make room for peaceful jubilation. Vlad fell back onto his pillow, smiling at the ceiling, and fondling images shaped by the smooth curves of lingering emotion.

It was Sunday. Molly was probably on her way to Washington Square. He closed his eyes and slept until midafternoon. After he woke, he washed and went down to the street to find a restaurant. On the street, he turned away from the East River, not wanting to retrace his steps from the prior day.

He walked into a restaurant and sat at a table in the corner. A blackened brick wall supporting heavy pine rafters separated him from the sunlight that poured into the far side of the restaurant. The low light hovering over his side of the restaurant burned steadily in gas lanterns that hung from the rafters.

Vlad ate quietly, while methodically separating conversations from the resonant hum. In the sunlight across the room, a man in a black top hat stood smiling as he offered a toast. At the table next to Vlad, two men spoke of escaping on a train. The man doing most of the talking was heavier set and wore high-waisted pants held up with suspenders. His long beard exaggerated the motion of his jaw as he spoke. The other wore his coat buttoned up to his neck and sat chewing on a pipe beneath his mustache.

"I don't want to end up dead on the street," said the heavyset man, "like that fella whose body we saw lying in Paradise Square for two days."

Vlad allowed their conversation to fall back into the prevailing clamor, and tried to single out some other voice. He felt himself buckling under the weight of the low ceiling. Placing his silverware on the plate in front of him, he pushed his chair away from the table and stood up. Taking a deep breath, he sat back down and turned to the men beside him.

"How far do the trains go these days?" asked Vlad.

"I'm not sure," replied the heavyset man, appearing to take an interest in the question. "I know you can catch a steamboat at the Castle Gardens that'll take you to Piermont. From there you can take the Erie Railroad to Chicago."

"Thank you," said Vlad, standing to leave. He paid for his dinner and walked back down Mulberry Street, keeping his eyes on the ground until he reached the pier.

Sitting atop a row of wooden barrels that lined the railing of the pier, he leaned back and took in South Street. The bowsprit of a merchant ship jutted out over the street behind him, as though reaching for the brick facades that rose over the East River, disheveled tenements stacked high to afford inhabitants a view of the waters that had carried them there. On the ground, pedestrians filed around the buildings and into the street, pursuing affairs of trade along the pier.

He turned his attention to the tide breaking softly against the pier. He thought of Molly and the vulgarity of two free spirits shutting themselves up in an apartment. Should they manage to keep the air in his apartment fragrant for a time with the flame of romance; his balcony was not high enough to escape the pervasive smell of mortality that rose from the Five Points. If there was any future for him, it was far from that slum of a neighborhood.

He tuned his ear to something beneath the wafting chatter of pedestrian traffic and further still beneath the clopping hooves atop the cobblestone. It was the sound of creaking lumber from the many ships that lined the pier and rocked in the same easy tide that held his gaze. He tried to memorize the sound, considering the likelihood that he would only hear it again in his memories.

Calling up memories was presently a thorny endeavor that involved foraging through lingering images of the nightmares that plagued his sleep. Just as he felt he would slip into despair from his thoughts, some men began loading a wagon with the barrels upon which Vlad was seated. Surrendering his position, he withdrew to the isolation of the crowds and made his way down the street. As he passed the place where he had seen the three boys resting in the narrow alley, he could not keep himself from looking back into that dreadful sarcophagus. The boys from the day before were gone, though three more children had taken their place, huddled above the sour grate. One of the children rested his head in the lap of a little girl who sat slouched in the corner, wearing a soiled bonnet. Vlad turned away quickly, nearly stepping in front of a horse drawing a wagon down the street. His heart beat quickly, and his eyes were glossing over.

At the boarding house, he ran up the stairs to his tenement. Before entering his room, he noticed the door opposite his. Desperation moved him to knock, assuming the door to be Molly's. He thought it odd that he had not questioned her about it the night before, after unintentionally stumbling through it, though that was a story he could not verify but for a loose deduction. When no one answered, he tried the doorknob, but it was locked.

In his room, he removed his coat and shoes, and crawled back into bed, marveling at the comfort one may find behind a shabby wooden door. He couldn't remember if he locked the door, and decided to check. It was not locked, and, thinking again of Molly, he left it that way. After crawling back under the covers, he ran his fingers over his shirt to find his mother's necklace and fell asleep to the recurring hum of the street below.

When he opened his eyes, it was night. Another candle had been lit, and he rolled over to find Molly sleeping next to him. He brushed her hair away from her face and her smile told him that he had woken her. She opened her eyes and kissed him. Her lips were a sweltering fury that burned away every contempt that might be held in life. They kissed until the embers of physical pleasure were smothered with the candle flame.

They held each other in the dark for a time; then Molly rose to light another candle. Vlad studied her back as she put out the match and reached to trace the image of her hip, running his finger through the cool air as she turned to find the covers. He wanted her again. "You," he said, shaking his head at her beauty.

"What?" she asked, giving him a sideways look.

"You are something," he said, taking a deep breath.

"No," she said. "You are. I should paint you again."

"If you like pictures of death," began Vlad, "I have the perfect scene for you, three new sitters. Tomorrow, cross the street and head for the pier. You'll not go far, before you come to a narrow alley where children lay in filth atop an iron grate, restrained in peaceful slumber, waiting for death to reach up from the foul pit and steal whatever chance they have left. Perhaps the aristocracy is content to sacrifice the children of this city to the god of death, though it is surely because they do not have to look at it. You could make them see it. You could hang the affliction of this place in paintings all over Murray Hill."

"No one will pay any attention to a painting of vile decay," said Molly. "They want to see the pale beauty of a cursed youth casually flirting with dark angels."

"Are we not all flirting with dark angels?" asked Vlad.

"But you make it look enviable," said Molly.

"If that is true," he said, "then my appearance betrays me. I would give anything to lift this curse."

"Curses are intriguing," said Molly, playfully.

"Is that why you are in my bed?" asked Vlad, yielding to Molly's banter with a smile.

"Yes," exclaimed Molly. "You are intriguing." She squinted at him. "And handsome. There is an innocence about you."

"And you would steal it from me?" jested Vlad.

"I don't want to steal it," said Molly. "I only want to hold it for a while."

"I'm sorry to disappoint you," said Vlad, "but there is nothing innocent about me."

"I don't believe you," said Molly. "You're nice." Her eyes lowered to his chest. "Most of the men I know are not so nice."

"What about your doctor friend, Edwin?" asked Vlad. "Is he not nice?"

"Edwin is not a doctor," she replied. "He thinks he deserves me, but I am indebted to no one."

Vlad was not sure how to reply.

"Are you really going to chance the Oregon Trail to find the doctor Edwin mentioned?" asked Molly.

"Gordon Newhall," answered Vlad. "Yes. I am leaving in the morning."

Molly's eyes glassed over, as though she were lost in thought, but quickly returned to Vlad under his inspecting gaze. She smiled and stretched her neck to kiss him, then tucked her forehead under his chin. He found repose in the warmth of her breath against his chest. He closed his eyes and felt himself fading beneath the veiled glow of candlelight and the steady breathing of his lover.

Molly was gone when he woke in the morning. In her place lay an older revolver bundled in a shoulder harness. He sat up, spurred by anxiety, and stumbled out of bed as if to correct his incriminating posture of lying next to a stolen artifact.

He moved to gather his clothes and his thoughts. Perhaps, he was jumping to the wrong conclusion, and it was not the prized property of Molly's employer lying on his bed. He put on his pants and stood over the bed, unraveling the harness that sheathed the gun. His eyes widened as he examined the engraving on the revolver's handle. It was the same as the engraving on his mother's necklace. He could tell from the wear that the marking was not new.

He slid his arm into his coat as he stepped into the hall, not bothering to put on a shirt, and began knocking on the door opposite his, realizing that he had forgotten to ask Molly if it was in fact her door. When no one answered, he tried the doorknob, but it was locked, as before.

Back in his room, he stopped at the sight of the cold revolver lying on his bed, as though he had happened upon a snake sunbathing in his path. He could leave it as he'd found it, and back away, but it was Molly's farewell gift to him, and he wanted it. The mysterious engraving that linked it to his past, along with the fact that it was stolen, was both disturbing and fascinating.

When he had finished washing and dressing, he removed his coat to slip the holster over his shirt. The weight of the gun was comforting, like Molly's hand against his chest. It wasn't as though it could be undone. The revolver was the *corpus delicti* of Molly's crime, and he was going to take it far from that scene.

Securing his things, he thought of the mask in his bag. It too had belonged to another when he had taken it. He assured himself the comparison was unfair, and locked the door behind him. In front of Molly's door, he contemplated knocking one last time, but continued to the stairs. After returning his key to the clerk, he stepped out into the street and turned his back on the shanty building that he might have called a home.

His pace quickened, and he tested the air for a scent of adventure. Perhaps it was there mixed with the familiar smell of death. He recognized only the same sour wind that often startled him from better thoughts, whispering its exhortation of mortality. Nevertheless, his luggage felt lighter, and his chest filled with air as he floated along examining the prospect of a new adventure.

It wasn't until he neared the Castle Gardens and saw the steamboats over the wharf that he began to feel something weighing him down. His thoughts brushed by the mask buried in his luggage, and the gun across his chest felt as light as samurai armor. The heavy weight seemed to come from inside, deep in his gut, memories scored like serrated stones that he had been forced to swallow. He had left them there, growing heavier with time. To look to the west was to look back, a temptation he had managed to evade.

CHAPTER FOUR

BRANCHES OF BILLOWY OAK trees waved to the rail cars that barreled down the track toward Chicago. Vlad looked out the train window in a sleepy daze. Somewhere beyond the oaks was the southern shore of Lake Erie. He could not make out the water, though judging by the sky and the movement of the trees, he imagined a frothy blanket of waves tamed only by a distant horizon beyond his view.

Presently, the only horizon in sight stretched across memories from a life that grew distant as quickly as the train pushed westward. When he closed his eyes, he lost himself in the steady rumble of locomotion. He pretended that he could feel the Earth rotate. While he longed to find comfort in anticipation of a new dawn, he was left clinging to memories that slipped into the darkness beyond the horizon.

He closed his eyes again and allowed his thoughts to take him back to the Tōkaidō Road, another adventure that had left him to walk alone in a new direction. He remembered that morning as though it were yesterday. That morning, everyone seemed to have fled the Tōkaidō Road, like startled fish scattering from the kill. His companion was dead. Vlad had followed him, because of the man's nose for adventure, though friendship would forever remain a milestone beyond their exploits. A man of disrepute, his temperament left a taste too foul for even the most underdeveloped palate. His hubris finally overwhelmed him. In Bangkok, it had managed to land them on a US Consul's ship bound for Shimoda, it had chased them from Shimoda to Nagasaki, and before they could make it back, the man's pretension had caught and killed him. Vlad was left to follow a corpse to the grave.

Only a wall of heavy fog stood before him as he led his horse through the corridor of dense pines. Blood still flowed from the body of his late companion, draped over the horse. It dripped from the horse's hair and traced a path toward Shimoda.

He glanced down at the swords tied to his belt. Both clung to him like a sharp anxiety that he had fastened too tightly around his waist. He had not taken them for a sense of comfort. It was a sense of survival that compelled him. It no longer mattered if it was worth the risk, for he could not bring himself to part with them.

Looking up, his eyes widened as he watched a rider's horse step through the fog ahead. His impulse was to pull the horse into the leafy brush that crowded the tall pines, but the fog had stolen the opportunity. The rider was already too close.

If Vlad had to meet anyone, he had hoped they would be on foot. Commoners would be less likely to interfere. He led the horse as far to the side as he could, then stopped to bow. Staring blankly at the smooth stones beneath his feet, he could see in his periphery that the rider had stopped as well. He began to feel his heartbeat, but he dared not reach for a sword.

He breathed a sigh as the rider drove his horse onward, but the breath was cut short by a blow to his shoulder. The rider dismounted his horse and delivered the blow with his foot, all in one motion. Vlad fell backward into the brush and quickly rolled to his feet.

"Where did you get those swords?" demanded his assailant.

"From a samurai," he answered, still not daring to reach for a sword. He kept his hands in the air as he inched back onto the road.

"A samurai gave them to you?" questioned his assailant, more sternly than before.

"No," said Vlad, feeling compelled to answer, though fear cautioned him against it. "I killed him."

His words appeared to strike the assailant, who stepped back and grasped the hilt of his katana. Vlad followed suit, grasping both swords. The assailant drew his long sword, and by the time he had wrapped both hands around the hilt, Vlad was wielding a katana and his short sword.

Vlad pointed the katana at his assailant's face and held the shorter wakizashi in his off hand. He stared obscurely at the assailant, maintaining a broad gaze as though peril might strike from any angle.

"You have studied The Book of Five Rings," said the assailant, eyeing him in disbelief.

"I do not understand," returned Vlad.

"How do you know Niten Ichi-ryū?" questioned the assailant.

"I do not know him," said Vlad.

"It is a school," the assailant told him, "not a man. What is your name?"

"Samatsu," answered Vlad.

The assailant squinted at him. "Where did you get this name?" he asked, at last.

"It was given to me," he said. "What is your name?"

"Shimazu Gensai," said the assailant. "Why did you kill a samurai?"

Holding his gaze, Vlad pointed his wakizashi at the body draped over the horse. "He killed this man," he told Gensai, adding, "my companion. And he tried to kill me."

"Why?" asked Gensai.

"My companion did not yield the road," replied Vlad.

"It was the samurai's right to avenge his honor," argued Gensai.

There was a long pause as the two held their gaze and their swords. A strong wind blew in from the south, stirring up dust and leaves, which danced around the combatants. The tall pines swayed overhead, wrestling a glimmer of light from the grey canopy. For only a moment, the assault on his senses caused Vlad to feel something he had not felt in a long time. Not at home, for home was merely a vague sentiment he fancied in the sustained moments of profound insight, or warm memories, though perhaps they were one and the same. The present feeling was similar, but he would draw out a contention that he was at peace.

His heart stopped with the wind, as his eyes fought to reacquire the gravity carved into the still air by the suspended blades. His eyes flashed to those of his opponent, and he was certain that Gensai had seen where he'd gone.

"Where is the samurai?" asked Gensai.

"They took him," said Vlad.

"Who?" pressed Gensai.

"I do not know," Vlad assured him.

"Where are you going?" asked Gensai, sliding his sword back into its wooden sheath.

"Shimoda," replied Vlad, cautiously lowering his swords.

"It's too far," insisted Gensai, "you'll never make it." He paused for a few moments, as though contemplating, then began again. "Will anyone come looking for your companion?"

It took some time for Vlad to absorb the words. Gensai pointed to the body.

"No," answered Vlad, finally.

"Come with me," said Gensai, "I will show you where to bury him."

He returned each sword to its saya, as Gensai had done, though without the same grace that had spoken of Gensai's mastery. His movements did not appear to go unnoticed by Gensai, who stood in curious observation before turning back to his horse. Vlad watched as the samurai mounted his horse. Gensai urged the horse forward a step and turned to look back at Vlad.

Vlad looked ahead to the wall of fog. Gensai was right, of course, even if he could not see its face through the fog, he knew it was a champion of doom that descended from the mountains to the east. However, it was not the only face hidden in the fog. He would have to look for the face of hope on Gensai's shoulders if he were to follow him back down the trail of blood.

Vlad watched his memory of the Tōkaidō Road flash by like the scenery outside the window of his passenger car. Despite his travels, he always ended up in the same place, attempting to find some aim that might lure him steadily down a clear path.

Sufficiently disoriented by the novelty of this latest adventure, he had yet to experience any loneliness, though as Molly passed through his thoughts he became aware of the seeds of this burden, which he expected to take root when the time was ripe. Presently, he considered the weight of a more familiar burden, as he examined the locket in his hand.

His sister, Laila, had given the locket to him at Mullanphy Hospital when they were children. Once cholera began to take even the Daughters of Charity, little hope remained for Laila. He had never intended on returning to St. Louis, but Laila's grave stood in the gateway to the West.

His eyes traced the lines of the engraving on the locket. The locket was his mother's, and after her death, Vlad's father gave it to Laila. He wondered if the ride west might stir up some childhood memory, all but lost, and likely for the better. He had come to wonder if even the shadow of their father, which sometimes passed through his thoughts, was tethered to any true recollection, or if it was merely a ghost of his own design. Any mention of Indians would invariably summon that specter of a notion that he could only refer to as his father's ghost, yet there were no memories to tie one to the other, aside from vague explanations given him as a child by the Daughters of Charity.

Attempting to conjure any memory of Indians merely summoned the images of war-painted caricatures, warriors masking themselves with paint and relics of the animals they had hunted. His mind wandered as he contemplated the intent of their costume, and he decided that it was to strike fear in the hearts of their enemies. He knew that the samurai class of Japan wore masks to evoke fear in battle, but those elaborate masks also served as armor.

The familiar devilish features of the mask he carried had roused him from his sleep earlier. He assured himself there was no air to breathe in the sleeper car, but the lingering image of the mask threatened to strangle him even after he had returned to his seat in the passenger car. And Death's lustful eyes, dark and menacing, glowed hotter behind another facade, the mask that he had called life, beautiful, disturbing. Still, he could not look away from the masquerade. It seemed a terrible mistake, for the great mystery was never in the mask, but in what lay behind it. Death is a punctuation mark, he thought, explicitly imposing, but not mysterious.

He felt as though he had stumbled upon something here among his thoughts, upon some significance, which he suspected to be near the source of a curse that plagued him. Need death impersonate something more terrifying? Had death any use for armor? What was the purpose of that mask of a life, which rose like the sun to paint an illusion of permanence in a world that merely spun itself back into the darkness from which it came?

After examining the revolver again, he had left it on the seat beside him. Taking notice of it once more, he looked for some significance in the fact that the train was carrying him to a destination that he had chosen, and the dark thoughts that he had elected to entertain had carried him to a gun, but he was surprised to find only intrigue in the object itself.

He imagined one of the Daughters of Charity arguing with him that a weapon is not the sort of thing for which a person should maintain an affection. He allowed his thoughts to argue back that the Earth spans many worlds and many ways of looking both inward and outward. He had learned, for instance, that a sword could be viewed in a way that was spiritual.

The revolver was no sword, but it was intriguing. He envisioned its density as a metaphor for its singular purpose, such a heavy object weighed down by a moral of caution. Its mechanics were the art of ingenuity, and the engraving on the handle was evidence of a mystery. He noted the peculiarity of the engraving on a locket and a revolver, an image that otherwise had no meaning, an impossible riddle.

Lifting the revolver, he returned it to the holster beneath his lapel. He sat still for a moment noting the feeling of it against his chest. He found it odd, but he was sure he breathed easier beneath its weight.

"The West," he spoke aloud. Perhaps it was his romantic disease that tempted him with a vision of riding out to meet his fate, but he did not hold heroism among his good qualities, if he would presume to hold any. He was not interested in a good death. While death is a stone left unturned by all who gaze upon it, it seemed to him that most who looked saw something through a conviction that granted a kind of stoicism. To some, death was a doorway to a new life, or an honor to be achieved in battle, while to others it was simply an abrupt end.

It was the latter that he could not reconcile. He simply would not accept a presumption that stripped all meaning from life. He knew he must go to the grave, but he could not consent, knowing that it would take everything from him. In the heat of the moment he knew he could act like a samurai, ignoring the question of victory or defeat, and charge daringly toward an irrational death, yet life was more than a moment. He felt as though he lacked a certain understanding that might grant him the resolve to accept his death, a vision that would give him the upper hand.

Subtle and mysterious so that he might control the fate of his opponent, this was a simple creed from the last remnants of anything he might call faith. His dreams were a descent into the abyss that loomed beneath the crumbling surface of his life. Yet, he had managed to pass another day clinging to the land of the living. If life were simply a mask, a prize commensurate with the chance to wear it, then he would teach death an eternal lesson in patience.

CHAPTER FIVE

MORNING CAME TO QUINCY with the sound of steamboats whistling on the Mississippi River. Vlad pulled back the curtains of a tall window, and watched as an image of the devilish red samurai mask, which had chased him from his bed, dissolved in the sunlight that flooded the room. A flourishing transportation hub, the river city of Quincy was built atop bluffs overlooking the Mississippi. Squinting through the window, Vlad could see down to the river where distant steamboats were docking at the landing.

Time was passing quickly, and the days were beginning to blur together. What little he had seen of Chicago from the train had floated away atop endless miles of oats and corn. A thousand miles lay between him and the Port of New York, where he had last seen a clipper sailing out into the upper bay. Halfway to his destination, a thousand miles remained to test the stubbornness of hope.

He sat on a chair beside the bed and rubbed his eyes. Death had long since haunted his dreams, but only recently had it begun to wear the mask.

Thinking he heard a familiar voice, he listened as someone made his way down the hall outside the door.

His curiosity drew him closer to the door, and he peaked out to see an older man in a dark, fitted frock coat carrying a suitcase. He watched until the man began to turn back toward him, then he shut himself back in his room and began to dress and gather his things. There was nothing familiar in the man's face, but Vlad could swear he had heard the voice before.

Upon leaving the hotel, Vlad boarded a steamboat headed for Hannibal, Missouri. The boat was a sternwheeler, as its paddle wheel was positioned in the back. At roughly a hundred feet long, the main deck extend out ahead of the boiler deck at the bow, where Vlad stood looking up at the two chimneys, which rose high above the hurricane deck in front of the pilothouse.

The steamer had not gone far on the river before the vessel began navigating debris, which Vlad soon learned was the remnants of another steamer that had been wrecked only recently. Its boilers had exploded, sinking the vessel and taking several passengers along with it. Passing several smaller boats, Vlad could see that a large effort was still underway to retrieve cargo from the sunken steamer.

Vlad crossed to the other side of the boat to inspect the debris. He noted that while most of the passengers were leaning over the rail as he was, eager to observe the catastrophe, standing apart from the rest was the older gentleman with the familiar voice from the hotel. He was surrounded by a small group of individuals engaged in conversation. Vlad moved closer to hear the man's voice.

"They wanted to make me the marshal," said the man, "but I had already rounded up all the outlaws in town."

"What did you do with them?" asked one of the men circled around him.

"One of them thought to pull his gun before the idea of surrender crossed his mind," answered the man from the hotel. "I shot him. The others might as well have gone down shooting. The town saw them hanged in the end."

"Why didn't you want to be marshal?" asked another of the bystanders.

"I'm not about to sit around in a town with no outlaws and let Pinkerton have all the fun," was the reply. This drew laughter from the man's audience, though it sounded like a forced gesture, a polite concession to common etiquette.

Vlad went on listening as best he could for a time, though his attention soon shifted to the gossip that began to circulate among the other passengers regarding the captain of the sunken vessel. The predominant assumption was that he was blown to shore by the blast, and his body found headless.

Vlad forced his attention to the far bank where limestone bluffs towered in the distance. The great white faces of the bluffs stood like castle walls, pushing through the trees, refusing to be concealed. They were giant earthen sentinels from another age, guarding the waters that slowly returned those lands to the sea. In spite of the captivating scenery, he found it difficult to think of anything but the headless body of the luckless steamboat captain.

Below Quincy, standing at the first bank that descended from the bluffs, which guard Missouri's northern prairie, was Hannibal, a bustling town that had become a regional center for the trade of livestock and grains. The town rose along a valley and up the side of a bluff, overlooking the river. Not far from the bank was the railhead of the Hannibal and St. Joseph Railroad. Vlad boarded a train bound for St. Joseph, and soon it was steaming up through the valley to the level prairie.

Like the train-coach cars that had carried him to Chicago and Quincy, the passenger car was a long cabin with rows of benches and a door at either end. He took the first available seat, next to a man who was removing the collar from his shirt. The man had already removed the stud from the front of his collar. When Vlad sat down, the man was reaching behind his head to work the back stud free from the tunic. Having finished, he pulled the collar free and lowered his arms so that Vlad could see his face. Immediately, Vlad found himself wondering if he would have preferred the man to have removed his head instead, and revealed himself as the doomed steamboat captain who'd been blown to shore near Hannibal.

"Ben Ferriday," exclaimed the man, extending his hand to Vlad. His voice still carried a familiar tone.

It was the older man he had first seen at the hotel, and then again on the steamboat. Vlad quickly dismissed the temptation to ascribe this chance meeting to destiny. He sat up straight and gave Mr. Ferriday his name in return, then leaned over to shake his hand. "You're the bounty hunter," he said, pausing briefly in the event that Mr. Ferriday should reply, but moved quickly to explain himself. "I overheard you speaking to someone on the steamer."

"I prefer *outlaw* hunter," Mr. Ferriday replied. "Though, I'm no Pinkerton. A Pinkerton is required to refuse a reward, a statute I find most disagreeable." He laughed at himself and made light of a notion that he could not abide with a single statute of Pinkerton's code.

Vlad gave a quick smile in acknowledgment and then turned to cough. After gaining his composure, he sank back into his seat, turning slightly toward the aisle. Mr. Ferriday began speaking again, undeterred by Vlad's convulsive scene.

"There's a book called *The Nicomachean Ethics* by the Greek philosopher Aristotle—"

"I have read it," interrupted Vlad, eager to avoid any explication from Mr. Ferriday, yet he was somewhat surprised at its mention.

"Is that so?" asked Mr. Ferriday. "Do you recall the analogy of the harpist?"

Mr. Ferriday's demeanor suggested that the question was asked in sincere interest, though Vlad still felt as though he was being tested.

"The analogy between a harpist and a good harpist, yes," he replied. "It is used to demonstrate a difference in quality, whereupon Aristotle advances to show that every activity varies in quality below some archetypical good."

"That's right," said Mr. Ferriday outwardly pleased with the answer. "It goes to show that a good life is not something that one has, but that one does. One gains a good life no more easily than one becomes a good harpist."

Vlad gave another quick smile of acknowledgment and attempted to turn back to the aisle.

"So you are dying," Mr. Ferriday continued. "What does it matter?"

Forcing his attention back to Mr. Ferriday, Vlad attempted not to appear disturbed, though he half expected the man to at last remove his head.

"The whole world is dying," Mr. Ferriday went on. "Soon there will be no frontier left, and man's only hope for true happiness will be ground up under his own plow."

He spoke with a dramatic flair, and had he not already revealed his profession, Vlad thought he would likely have attributed this to an extraordinary religious fervor, or thought him a man gone slightly mad. As to the latter, he decided that he would maintain his suspicion.

Mr. Ferriday's proclamation about happiness was only the beginning of a dissertation that unexpectedly moved to the subject of zoos and the business of zookeepers. "It is imperative," he said, "that zookeepers succeed in recreating an animal's natural habitat in order to sustain the animal in captivity. If the zookeeper does not succeed in doing so, the animal will not be happy, and, consequently, will not survive being held in captivity. What do you think is mankind's natural habitat?"

Vlad looked undecidedly at Mr. Ferriday, angry that he felt compelled to answer in spite of every desire to be done with the man's exposition. "I couldn't say," he muttered.

"As animals ourselves," continued Mr. Ferriday, "how can we expect to be truly happy unless we learn to abide in our natural habitat?" He paused for effect, before proceeding to expound upon the suggestion implicit in his rhetoric. "The West bears the last example of mankind in his natural habitat. You can observe the Indians, roaming about, accepting what nature gives, and warring with others in order to maintain an equilibrium. It's in sharp contrast to the present where mankind toils his life away working the land for no other purpose than to offset the equilibrium, so that we may go about believing that a good life is equal simply to more life."

By 'more life', Vlad understood him to mean longer life, but he did not want to indicate any interest by asking for clarification.

"It's a messy picture, now," said Mr. Ferriday, "The equilibrium is out of balance in more ways than one. This creates a need for someone like me, someone willing to cut down the underbrush that is rising up to slow the road to conquest and threatening the new *good* life. The irony is that there's no reason to fear war or death. They are a natural part of life, yet we build fences, and inside our houses we pretend we can shut out the natural world that bore us."

Vlad was about to suggest that fear was also a natural part of life, but held his tongue and assured himself that this was not a man with whom he wished to engage in a discussion. However, he found himself curious as to the nature of the underbrush that Mr. Ferriday had referred to. His mind began searching for the ambit of behavior that might earn one the mark of an outlaw, and his thoughts trailed off, until Mr. Ferriday addressed him personally.

"You're no longer at liberty to maintain that common expectation that tempts us to forsake the present moment," suggested Mr. Ferriday.

Vlad nodded, glancing at Mr. Ferriday from the corner of his eye. He needed no clarification in understanding Mr. Ferriday's meaning, that the inevitable brevity of his life should prevent him from getting lost in the future. "I suppose you are right," he replied vaguely. He turned away, trying to breathe out the heat that was welling up from within. His thoughts were being churned up in a whirlpool of anxiety. The more he fought to calm himself, the faster his heart beat. He was sweating and, in a panic, he stood before realizing he had nowhere to go.

"Are you alright?" asked Mr. Ferriday.

"Yes," Vlad heard himself say as he glanced hazily about the car. It seemed he had been convinced by his own remark, for he began to breathe easier and a sudden calm came over him. A barrage of impressions flooded his senses as he returned to his seat, a stockpile of perception previously congested by the barrier of anxiety that had forced the air from his lungs. The passengers around him stood out in greater clarity. He could smell them, see the lines in their skin; he could feel their presence.

Perhaps it was a will to find some cause for empathy that led him to the suspicion that Mr. Ferriday's inquiries were motivated by a need to reconcile some anxiety, possibly a conflicting conscience. Killing people is disconcerting, he thought, even when it is justified. He had felt his own anxiety about death moving him to devour any philosophy, new or old, that he might encounter, in an attempt to ease the burden of dread. This was the case even before he found himself so near the end. He wondered if he were attempting to cloak Mr. Ferriday in his own inclinations for lack of another way of framing him. Perhaps the man was, in fact, slightly mad, he thought, and he considered the possibility that everyone might be a little mad. Nevertheless, he felt that Mr. Ferriday's intellectual front lacked an anchor. The man's discourse continued to drift, though, occasionally, he would say something that seemed to draw Vlad's attention against his will, like: "The idea of death is only upsetting if you believe there is some alternative, but there is not." Despite the man's bizarre straight-faced proposals and attempts to herd his wildly scattered submissions into a coherent line of reasoning, Vlad sensed some inherent wisdom in Mr. Ferriday's voice, and found it disconcerting. It was a kind of discomfort he would expect to feel when some circumstance came into question as a matter of carelessness, such as the sudden realization that he'd been walking in the wrong direction. However, his intuition assured him that this was no man to be taking directions from.

Genuine exchange was lost in Mr. Ferriday's performance, and Vlad regarded the entire encounter with distaste. He felt as though he was being evaluated in some way, and when he stood to retrieve his luggage, the feeling was bolstered by Mr. Ferriday's ensuing reaction.

With his arms raised to lower his luggage, the lapel of his coat had opened enough to reveal his holster. At the sight of Vlad's revolver, Mr. Ferriday jumped up, and his eyes widened. In an apparent state of shock, he left his mouth hanging open as he pushed his nose closer to Vlad's chest. Mr. Ferriday nervously slipped his hand into his coat. At the sight of the gesture, Vlad shoved the man to the floor and jumped in front of a group of passengers making their way down the aisle, quickly distancing himself from Mr. Ferriday. He convinced himself that he could hear the man's voice calling after him over the bustle of passengers eager to leave the car. Minding not to look back, he made his way onto the platform, and remained hidden among the crowds until he was able to board the train to St. Louis.

On board, he closed his eyes. The cars gained momentum, but he was unable to calm his mind. He became infatuated with scenarios that proffered a sum of wild explanations for Mr. Ferriday's behavior. These included an account wherein the stolen revolver was given as a form of identification to an outlaw hunter. As he neared St. Louis, the mystery proved so irritating that he found himself regretting that he hadn't simply thrown caution to the wind and confronted the man about his reaction. Instead, he was left to speculate about the affair, going so far as to wonder if he would now be required to evade some pursuit.

Looking out the window, he made an effort to compare the scenery to his recollection of the many sights he had witnessed since his departure from Manhattan. He regretted his oversight, wishing he had placed greater emphasis on considering what stood before him as opposed to what troubled him from within. It seemed he had lost the ability to hold on to anything good. Minding the current that swept him along his present course, it appeared that everything he set his eyes upon fled too quickly from his view. Trees, fields, rivers, mountains, the meaning behind such a brief life, an unusual name, a strange engraving, it all dissolved into the impeding darkness, hopelessly lost to a cursed fate.

His thoughts returned again to Mr. Ferriday, recalling that his acquaintance had confessed plans to continue on the central trail toward Salt Lake City. He tried to take comfort in the fact that he had not revealed his own intentions. Unless he entertained some fantastic probability that he was in fact being pursued, he might be able to console himself with the expectation that Mr. Ferriday was already far in advance of him, en route to Salt Lake City. Soon the pervasive nuisance of the mysterious reaction would fade, and he might yet hope to forget that he ever met Ben Ferriday.

CHAPTER SIX

ST. LOUIS WAS LITTLE more than a ferry ride in and out of St. Charles. Vlad's mind lingered in the sunny side of a field west of the city, focused on a tall tree in the distance. A collection of white stones stood under the shade of its great branches, apart from the rows of stones that ran the length of the field.

"It is the golden age of river traffic," he heard someone remark. He realized he was breathing heavily as the passenger's words ushered him back to the present. For Vlad, St. Louis was the gateway to something other than the West. A city wrapped in a river of memories that was navigated no more easily than the Big Muddy itself. After a few deep breaths, he dove back into the current of thought that ran dark, like the waters of the Missouri.

For the sake of expedience, he had avoided Spruce Street, though he wondered what childhood memories lingered there between the heavy brick walls of buildings inspired by the fire of '49. Mullanphy Hospital had narrowly escaped the flames, a fact often explained with an appeal to the notion of miracles.

He still had questions for Sister Caroline and the Daughters of Charity. He wanted to press her for answers as to why he was able to find no trace of his parents in Iowa. Only passive conjectures at the number of lives lost to the Sioux Indians. Presently, there were more immediate concerns, such as the whereabouts of the alleged Dr Newhall, and the hope of treatment.

The rails carried Vlad to St. Joseph, where he found himself boarding another steamer. It was built much like the Mississippi steamer, with the exception of having paddle wheels positioned on the sides of the vessel. While waiting to board, he had overheard the captain boasting that a sidewheeler was better suited for the Missouri River, due to its superior maneuverability.

After the steamer had embarked, Vlad fell asleep in his seat and dreamt of exploding boilers and sinking ships. His dreams hurled him into the muddy Missouri where he found himself treading with one arm. His other hand grasped his luggage, which threatened to pull him beneath the surface. As the weight grew heavier and he began to slip into the dark water, he realized he was fighting a losing battle, but he could not let go.

The water filling his lungs began to taste of blood, and he woke gasping for air. He looked around for some bearing outside of his dream. The steamer's boilers had not blown and no one had been spilled into the Missouri. Most of the passengers were focused on the distant shore, scanning for the source of an imposing resonance, which Vlad recognized as the sound of a firearm being discharged.

His waking fit attracted the attention of a couple sitting near to him. Between them sat a young boy who appeared as more of a specter than Vlad. Having been told that drier air was a common appeal for many migrants heading west, he assumed consumption was driving the boy's parents on a similar flight as his own. It occurred to him that ever since he had stepped away from the pier in the Five Points, he looked to the West with an almost mystical expectation, and when he tried to imagine the same view through the eyes of the boy's parents, he saw only naivety.

Vlad tried to imagine that the boy was someone dear to him, and that he had known him at a time when his face still held some color. He thought he would try to remember him that way even after the boy was gone. It made him sad to see the boy as he was now, a shadow with one foot in the grave, his own shadow perhaps. Suddenly, he feared being caught with the same pitiful look on his face.

He peered over the railing into the water below, but the dense silt obstructed any view of the river's bottom. This quality, he overheard another passenger explain, along with the river's indefinite rises and falls, contributed to the short life of ships in those waters.

Further down the Missouri, the ghostly boy passenger appeared to take an interest in Vlad's luggage.

"Do you like it?" He asked the boy. It was a long bag with thick leather sides that opened at the top like a Gladstone. In addition to the leather handles, a strap was fastened to metal D rings at either end, which allowed the bag to be slung over the shoulder. He explained that he had acquired it on one of his adventures. "It was given to me by a French doctor." The boy looked to Vlad, then back at the curious medical relic. Vlad supposed that to a young boy, the appearance of such an unusual pack could only start the imagination in pursuit of whatever unusual treasures might be bundled up inside.

Vlad opened the bag, and removed a small sword. "This is called a wakizashi. It is sometimes used to take one's own life as a matter of honor." He emphasized the word 'honor', using his voice in an attempt to spur the boy's fascination, and he thrust the sword toward his abdomen to illustrate. He smiled at the boy, but noticed the boy's mother had placed her hand on him. Vlad looked up to the mother and the warmth of embarrassment rushed through his body. He realized that he had failed to consider the nature of his audience. The boy was stopped before he could finish asking why someone would attempt such a feat, and his parents stood up to usher him away.

Soon the steamer neared Atchison, Kansas, and the west bank of the Missouri rose high under blankets of trees. The bend in the river led him to imagine the high bank as forming a great arch, like that of a bow pointing its arrow to the West, and at the precise spot where an arrow comes to rest on a bow, the west bank was carved out, opening a window to the plains. This is where he found Atchison, nestled in the prairie among rolling swells that he was inclined, only after a moment's pause, not to describe as hills.

Disembarking from the steamer, Vlad traversed the main street in search of lodging, all the while keeping an eye out for the likeness of Mr. Ferriday among the crowds. The ground held enough moisture to keep the street firm, preventing the dirt from rising in pursuit of his stride.

He remained attentive to the handle of his revolver under the left lapel of his coat. He carried his luggage on his left shoulder and carelessly held his lapel with his right hand as he made his way down the street. His intention was to keep his hand as close to the revolver as possible without gesturing a threat or a dare.

Between two buildings, he could see to a yard in the back where a group of spectators circled two men. The two men were on the ground, and he was unable to ascertain whether they were engaged in play or something of a more serious nature. He thought they might be wrestling.

He turned ahead in time to avoid colliding with a couple of nicely dressed men who had stepped into the street in front of him. Looking up from the corner of his eye he began to make out the profile of the man nearest to him. All of the muscles in his body tightened, like an army regiment snapping to attention. His right hand closed firmly around the cold handle of his revolver, and as quickly as he had slipped his hand inside his coat, he withdrew it empty and raised a finger to scratch his nose.

"I beg your pardon," said Vlad to the man that he suddenly recognized as a stranger.

"Watch your step," ordered the stranger. He issued this with disdain, convincing Vlad of a desire to have avoided the burden of addressing him. Looking ahead, Vlad continued on his way.

"I may have greater difficulty forgetting Mr. Ferriday than I had hoped," he mumbled to himself.

At the edge of town, he spotted a group of people standing atop the high prairie looking west, waiting, he assumed, for the sun to set. Their occupation served well enough to entice Vlad to the top. He sat, leaning back on his luggage, and stayed a while to study the view. Covering the prairie below were parties of gold-seekers making up trains headed for Pike's Peak. Covered wagons moved out as far as he could see. A stream of white canvas trailed off into the red sunset, like the sails of a fleet of fishing boats heading off to friendly waters. The swells of the distant prairie pushed the tide of adventure to the shores of Atchison, where those below looked on with anticipation.

Perhaps it was his mood, but he looked with them and sensed only the peril lying in the dark shadows that reached for them from beyond the horizon. He began to feel what his eyes had set out to confirm. He had reached the West.

CHAPTER SEVEN

THE JOURNEY ACROSS the Great Plains had long since earned a reputation as a treacherous endeavor. Vlad saw the road as a strange corridor that seemed to elevate his disposition, not by improving his condition, but by overwhelming everything else. The landscape was cast in the darkest shades of both humankind and nature. He was tempted to lament that death had followed him there, though he decided it would be a bold undertaking. It was clear that death was no stranger to the road and did not discriminate with regard to company.

As for his company, Vlad was surprised to have rejoined the boy and his parents from the Missouri steamboat. They met again in Council Grove as passengers on the same express coach, a mud wagon, named for its lightness and consequent ability to pass over muddy roads. The box was covered by a canvas roof, and the sides were open with framing for windows, front and back, and doors in-between. Canvas curtains could be rolled down over the windows and doors, though Vlad preferred to leave his up to take advantage of the view. Inside the vehicle, the boy and his parents occupied the front bench, while

Vlad sat facing them in the back among the bags of mail, which were under the charge of the conductor. The conductor sat out front, in the box, with the driver at his side.

After managing some words with the boy's father, Vlad learned that their move was motivated, as he had supposed, by the dry air expected to cure the boy's lungs.

"The dry air will be good for him," said Vlad, addressing the boy's father. "I don't suppose you know of a physician by the name of Gordon Newhall?"

"I can't say that I do," replied the boy's father.

"I am told that Dr Newhall is setting up an infirmary in the mountains near Pike's Peak," said Vlad. "An infirmary dedicated to the sole purpose of treating consumption." He paused to observe the reaction of the boy's parents upon hearing this news. Though neither appeared impressed by the revelation, Vlad continued, undeterred. "Dr Newhall is looking for volunteers to undergo treatment, in order to test his prognosis. The alpine air is the key. That is where I am headed. Perhaps you would be interested in seeking treatment there for your son."

"I don't think so," replied the boy's father without hesitation. "I can't run cattle in the mountains."

As their conversation progressed, it was established that the boy's parents had come from a deeply religious merchant family back East. The man and his wife were on their way to manage a cattle ranch in Arizona that was making a fortune selling meat to the Overland Stagecoach Company. Vlad was surprised to find that the man refused to carry a gun.

"I've heard that everyone in Arizona carries a gun," commented Vlad. "I've heard that it is necessary."

"I've never so much as fired one," declared the man. "I believe that any man who views a weapon as a necessity is surely looking to compensate for some other deficiency, even if he is unaware of it."

"What sort of deficiency do you mean?" asked Vlad, curious to learn if there was any substance to the man's claim, or if he was merely attempting to mask some deficiency of his own.

The man looked Vlad over for a moment before answering. "Grace, perhaps," he said, turning his head toward the window and looking up to the sky, as though to indicate he had dispensed with any affairs inside the coach. Vlad noticed the boy eyeing him, so he returned a smile, then leaned back on the mailbags and contemplated the scenery outside the far window.

The trail was surprisingly good for a natural road, winding over the high prairie as much as possible to avoid the low areas carved out by streams. After a brief stop at Diamond Springs to water the horses, they overtook a party of 'emigrants' as Vlad had heard them called, wagon trains of migrants heading west for a chance at a better life. As with many of the trains that

Vlad had encountered, every wagon was overloaded and many of the oxen appeared untrained. He marveled at the efforts required to keep such animals on the road, even as they were tethered to their heavy loads.

The progress of the trains was remarkably slow when compared with Vlad's coach, or with any means of transportation whatsoever. Initially, he had only imagined a more rapid advance on foot, and one of his drivers had since mentioned that many would indeed make the entire journey "under their own steam," as he put it. Since leaving Atchison, he had in fact witnessed many emigrants on foot keeping pace with the oxen and wagons of their parties.

Having made their way through the caravan, the speed of Vlad's stagecoach quickly outpaced the weary step of the oxen, and they found themselves alone on the open road. Unaware of any menacing presence that might have studied their route, in the same way that the grey wolf eyed the straggling calf of the herd, Vlad was struck by the realization that his coach had strayed from the others, banishing any safety in numbers to the dust of their tracks.

As if on cue, his acknowledgment was met by the sharp crack of a gunshot that rang out over the turbulence of the stagecoach. Debris from the door frame traced the trajectory of a ball, which just missed the boy's head. His mother doubled over wailing, and cupped her brow with her hands, which quickly drew the attention of her husband.

"Are you alright?" he shouted over the ensuing gunfire. "Let me see."

Sobbing, the man's wife lifted her head slightly. There was blood in one of her hands, and at the sight of it, she resumed her wailing and buried her face back into her palms.

The boy's teeth were clenched and his eyes were focused somewhere on the wall behind Vlad. He thought the boy looked as though he longed to cry, if only someone could assure him that it was alright to do so. He grabbed the boy by the shoulder of his coat and pulled him onto the floor.

The conductor's Sharps rifle fired atop the coach. This was the only shot from the box before the coach veered and nearly toppled on its side. For a moment they rode on but two of their wheels. Through the window, Vlad saw the driver's arm dangling so that his fingers nearly touched the ground, and just as he thought they would, the Sharps rifle hit the dirt instead, and the coach was righted.

Vlad assumed that the driver had been shot, and the now unarmed conductor had taken the reins. There was a fierce jolt when the other two wheels of the coach hit the ground, which made the boy cry out. The boy's father looked up at Vlad. The man had draped himself over his wife, who kept her head between her knees, still cupping her brow. He stared at Vlad for a moment as though waiting for an answer to some question of urgency.

Vlad pulled the revolver from his coat and turned around to take aim through the window. No sooner had he looked over the barrel, than two men came into focus riding side by side. The rider on the far side was taking aim with a revolver, and the rider nearest him appeared to have just finished reloading a shotgun. Vlad aimed at the rider nearest him and pulled the trigger.

The near rider's head whipped back from the concussion of the ball, which tore through the other side of his neck. The result of the shot was horrific. His jaw came unhinged on one side, lending an exaggerated appearance to his cry. A thick stream of blood issued forth like a rope pulling the man from his horse by his neck.

As he fell, his shotgun discharged in close proximity to the rider at his side. The other rider took this shot to his head, which came apart like a melon dropped on a stone. Their horses were turned abruptly into one another, which formed a barricade for a third rider that Vlad had not seen.

The third rider came upon the calamity of his fallen associates too quickly to react and was thrown over the front of his horse. His face met the ground first, and his legs continued forward over his back until he snapped into a position that appeared to have compromised the integrity of his body. He did not move once his body came to rest. No one moved, and everything, including the coach, came to a halt.

Vlad studied himself for a moment, wondering if this was when he might wake and realize that these were merely terrible visions from another one of his dreams. What a catastrophe he had spawned from a single shot. The curse of his infernal consumption had been cast into a single lead ball. He wished that it was only a dream, but if it was, he was unable to wake from it. It appeared to him that death had escaped the recent confines of his dreams, returning to haunt him once again in broad daylight.

Vlad set the boy back in his seat, next to his mother. "Is she alright?" Vlad asked her husband.

The man urged his wife to sit back and let go of her face. She had managed to calm herself, but her face wrinkled as she looked again at her bloody hands. Vlad leaned closer and saw that she had a cut above her eye. He assumed she had caught a piece of the debris from the door frame, which had been fragmented and scattered by the initial shot fired at them.

"You will be fine," Vlad tried to comfort her. "It's only a small laceration. You were quite lucky."

The woman looked up at him as though she were appalled by the suggestion.

Sincerity received out of turn was something Vlad had little patience for. "If you had caught the debris any lower," he said, turning to the door, "it is likely that you would have lost your eye."

Vlad was eager to get his feet on the ground, for the ride was not easy, even when the coach was riding on all four wheels. He was met by the conductor as he pushed aside the canvas curtain covering the door and was surprised to see the driver standing with him.

"I assumed you were a casualty," Vlad began in addressing the driver. "I saw you hanging from the box."

It was explained that during the conductor's struggle to engage their enemy, he became careless with his elbows and recklessly struck a blow to the driver's ear, all but knocking him from the coach.

Now, the conductor stood before Vlad. His eyes were wide and appeared to demand something. Vlad had to persuade him with the curtain to move back so that he could step down from the coach. After he had planted his feet on the ground and mustered a stretch to relieve his back, the conductor questioned Vlad. "What are you carrying?" he asked. His eyes glanced to Vlad's seat in the coach and then returned again to scan his hands and waist. It was this that prompted Vlad's recognition of his meaning. He appeared bent on identifying the weapon that had managed to effect such devastation.

"You are inquiring about my revolver," he replied.

"Revolver?" shouted the conductor, with surprise.

Vlad opened his coat with the intent of clearing up the matter and tapped his finger on the handle.

The conductor squinted at the revolver, proffered a foul glare, and held out his hand. "Let me have a look at that," he said.

"You'll have to forgive me," replied Vlad, "but I am rather particular about anyone handling it."

The conductor reacted with a grunt. He then ordered the driver to stay with the coach, and requested that Vlad follow him. He and the conductor made their way back toward the fallen men. As they walked, the conductor glanced nervously to the north and then to the south. He continued this until he noticed that his behavior had attracted Vlad's attention.

"Indians," explained the conductor. "They're known to raid this section of the road." Vlad could see that the concern weighed heavily on him. At one point during their jaunt, the conductor's body stiffened and he stood motionless glaring into the distance. He claimed to have observed something stir to the north, though Vlad could not confirm it.

As they approached the spot where the three riders lay, Vlad's eyes began to water, and his skin burned as though he were nearing a great blazing fire. He stopped and looked back to the stagecoach.

"What is your intention in coming back here?" Vlad asked, turning to the conductor.

"We're going to gather the guns and the horses," said the conductor, his tone suggesting impatience. "The wolves can have whatever the Indians don't want," he added, starting again toward the fallen riders.

"I'll retrieve those horses," said Vlad, motioning to two horses that had wandered further from the road. "I'll leave the guns to you."

He gathered the horses and led them back to the road, where he rejoined the conductor. Blood dripped from the hair of the horse the conductor led, and as Vlad stared, his thoughts returned to Shimazu Gensai and the Tōkaidō Road. He became aware of a devious question, demanding proof for the cursory assumption that there was nothing behind him. As he turned his head, he caught sight of something from the corner of his eye. He drew his revolver and spun around, aiming into a cloud of dust kicked up by the wind.

"What is it?" screamed the conductor hysterically.

Vlad returned his gun to its holster. The conductor had turned the bloody horse, and was standing behind it.

"Just the wind," said Vlad.

"Goddammit," shouted the conductor, "you scared the shit out of me."

They tethered the ruffians' horses to the back of the coach, and doubled back to retrieve the conductor's Sharps rifle. Alone on the road, the coach continued westward, until stopped by the fading light of a sunset that bled red as a reminder of the blood that had been spilled that day.

The coach would be their lodging for the night. Four men, a boy, and his mother, they now carried enough guns for all but one of their company, and a horse for each of their number, with one to spare. Were it not for his consumption, Vlad felt with some measure of confidence, the worst would have been behind him.

CHAPTER EIGHT

AFTER THE ENCOUNTER with the ruffians, the driver took an interest in his enigmatic passenger. Vlad was disturbed by the prior day's exceptional event, and perhaps equally disturbed by the driver's fascination with it. The other passengers were not so impressed with Vlad. The air in the coach was made colder by their diverted glances. He supposed, to them, he was but another shadow in the sinful darkness from which they prayed for deliverance.

He wondered if he, like the world's religious, was also looking for salvation. He supposed that everyone might be seeking something similar. He believed he would rest easy on his deathbed if he could ascertain some reason for the brevity of life. Presently rattled upon hardwood benches and wagon wheels, he feared the discomfort of a bed jolted by the rugged roads of a western trail.

Their progress on the road that day was halted by high winds and a need for rest. While they made camp, the conductor nervously scanned the horizon as he had done the day before. At that point on the trail, it was the prominence of cyclones that troubled him more than the Indians.

The coach was staked to the ground and the horses, trained to stay close, were turned loose. With the same misplaced grin that he wore when recounting the demise of the ruffians, the driver spun stories of whirlwinds that had taken wagons into the sky with their teams.

"It took the horses, too?" asked the boy.

"Sure enough," replied the driver. "It wasn't far from here, a man was driving a double team and a cyclone took the horses, wagon, man and all, up into the sky. Must have carried them a hundred rods or so before setting them back down."

"Were they hurt?" asked the boy.

His mother glanced at the driver, with a look of concern.

"No," exclaimed the driver, with excitement. "He drove the team back to the road and continued on his way."

The driver continued despite the frequent looks from the boy's parents. His stories included all manner of outcomes, some of which Vlad doubted, and none of which he would have mentioned in the company of the boy. He recalled with embarrassment his error on the Missouri steamboat, when he had used his wakizashi to illustrate a Japanese ritual suicide. The driver's stories did prove effective in persuading the boy's parents to make a bed on the ground with the rest of them, as they had meant to spend the night in the coach.

Vlad lay awake listening to the roaring of the wind. He found it comforting, and would have let it carry him off to sleep if he could only have let go of the desire to remain conscious of his contentment. Perhaps he had stumbled once again upon that brief sentiment, a feeling of home, or peace, and he did not want to let it slip through his fingers. He marveled at the idea that his warmest memories seemed to reside in the sound of the wind. Perhaps one day he would remember the roaring on the open prairie as a warm wind, the same that filled the sails of the *Magnificent* and stirred the sea of barley that led to the village where Shimazu Gensai had lived.

He assumed that the others were already asleep, but the sound of footsteps in the grass snuck in beneath the wind, and he lifted his head to make out a shadowy figure approaching. Judging by the stature, he knew it to be the boy. The boy stopped near Vlad and stood holding his bedding. It took no time for Vlad to perceive his intent, and he motioned for the boy to lie beside him.

After making his bed, the boy lay next to Vlad on his back, their ghostly white faces confronting the night sky. The boy said nothing and neither did Vlad, but his thoughts continued to ring out like the wind.

Here lay a boy who shared his fate. They had boarded the same black ship sailing steadily for the end of the world. Vlad had offered him some comfort, and he was surprised to find some comfort in the boy, even if it was merely the idea of him.

He wondered which was worse; dying from a disease or watching someone dear to him die from a disease. He didn't know what it was like to have a child, but he knew what it was like to have a sister. If the choice was his, of course, he would stay death's hunger with his own life, but such circumstances were not of his choosing. Still, there was an unexpected comfort in contriving circumstances where he might have chosen his present condition.

Vlad slept well that night, better than he had in quite some time. He was the last of the party to wake the next morning and could not recall a single dream. The others had risen, and the driver finished gathering the horses.

Vlad rolled over and began to cough as though he were compensating for what was long overdue. When he finished, he raised his head in time to catch a glance from the boy's mother before she could turn away. He realized his coughing fit was enough cause for attention, but he wondered if she was looking at him to catch a glimpse of the future. He was not as old as she, but he could not imagine her son living to reach even his own age.

After setting out that morning, they came upon another emigrant train still camped alongside the road. Vlad was charging the empty chamber of his revolver with powder when the boy mentioned some men were gathered in the road ahead. Vlad fought an inclination towards haste, and cautiously seated a ball and cap, before carefully lowering the hammer of his revolver. Looking out the window, he saw the men that the boy had spoken of. They appeared to bear no firearms, but still Vlad noted his consolation in having reloaded the empty chamber of his revolver. Soon the coach was brought to a halt, and Vlad listened as the men addressed the conductor.

While Vlad had passed the night in restful slumber, these emigrants had dwelt in fear. The wind had persuaded them to take precautions similar to Vlad's party, though their caution was met by an actual tornado.

Vlad stepped out of the coach as the men continued to tell of their misadventure. On the ground, he saw that a burial was the purpose of their convening in the middle of the road, and he listened with difficulty as one of the men explained.

"As soon as he jumped out of the wagon, the oxen were startled and pulled the wheel right over him. We had to chase them down to keep the dumb beasts from running off with the wagon."

It was not the first time he had heard of a man meeting his end under the weight of a wagon wheel. In accordance with what Vlad viewed as some dark irony, the man was buried in the middle of the road to make use of wagon wheels in compacting his grave. Not an uncommon practice, the aim, he was told, was to mask the scent, in order to prevent wolves from digging up the body. For all the bones he had seen lining the road, it was not difficult to understand that this was a legitimate concern.

The stranger's story of chasing down the wagon led to another story about a wagon that got away. "His mules were startled just like the oxen," began the stranger, "but they made off with the wagon, and there was no catching them. We still haven't found the mules, but we found the better part of the wagon on its side further down the road. Between all the wagons that were damaged, we were able to piece together all but one. Problem is, we no longer have a sufficient stock of animals to draw all the wagons. The storm took more than those mules that ran off."

"If it would help," Vlad interjected, "we picked up three horses along the trail."

The man looked at Vlad, and then to the back of the stagecoach. "Well, yes sir," he said, looking to the conductor for a confirmation of the offer.

The conductor shot a foul glare at Vlad. "What makes you think you've a right to be giving away the horses tethered to my coach?"

Vlad folded his arms. "Given the circumstances leading to our acquisition of those horses," he began, "I suppose I've the right to confer them. I might confer the remainder of the horses and the coach with them."

The conductor stood looking dumbfounded for a moment before settling back into his customary demeanor of disapproval.

"Perhaps you could arrange some compensation for the horses?" Vlad asked one of the emigrants.

The question led to diplomacy, and after an agreement was made, the conductor barked at the driver to loose the horses from the rear. Despite his agitated demeanor and his disregard for the bodies of the ruffians, Vlad chose to believe that the conductor was a good man.

All the passengers, except the boy's mother, took advantage of an opportunity to stretch their legs before continuing the journey. The timid woman could do no more than peek out beneath the curtains of the coach. When she saw the people standing around the grave in the middle of the road, she quickly withdrew from the window. The shadow of death still lingered, and Vlad understood if she preferred to remain hidden.

CHAPTER NINE

BACK ON THE ROAD, Vlad's coach was making good progress. It was not until he began to consider the effect of emigrant trains on their pace that they encountered another, and he began to wonder if he should have kept one of the horses for himself.

Wagons were stopped waiting for a stampede of bison, dark and disheveled, thundering across the road ahead. Some members of the party had ventured out in front with a rifle and were firing into the drove of great beasts. Upon hearing the gunshots, the driver decided to join them.

As Vlad stepped down from the coach, he heard the driver proposition the conductor in regard to the use of his rifle.

"What makes you think you can hit anything with it?" was the conductor's answer.

Moving up near the front boot, Vlad could not stop himself from interjecting. "He could certainly do no worse with the rifle than your display against the ruffians."

"Perhaps if you lend him your revolver," retorted the conductor, "he could bring down the whole herd!"

Vlad did not answer, and the conductor addressed the silence. "Nor, will he be using my rifle."

The driver tied the reins around the brake and jumped down from the box. "I guess I'll have to use the shotgun," he said, "or one of the revolvers that we took from those bandits."

"I think not," replied Vlad.

"You don't mean to lay claim to the guns as well," said the conductor angrily.

"I have no interest in those guns," replied Vlad, "though neither have I any interest in watching him injure those great beasts with no hope of bringing one down."

Listening to Vlad, the two seemed to exchange their prior dispositions. The driver appeared angry and the conductor confused.

By this time, a pair of emigrants had idled their way to the other side of the coach, seeking conversation with the conductor. They told how their lead wagon had been run off the road by the bison, but the driver had managed to safely turn the wagon in retreat, suffering only a scare.

Amidst their discourse, Vlad noted a reference to their guide as having recently spoken with a party of Indians. According to the men, the Indians had told their guide that the Devil was heading west on the same trail. This news was the cause of some trepidation among the emigrants.

"Where is your guide?" Vlad asked the men. One of them pointed to a swell of the prairie to the north, where Vlad was able to discern a man seated on the high ground. Without delay, he set out on foot with the intent of speaking to the guide.

He found the guide in a state of concentration, sketching on a piece of paper. The guide captured the scene before him, the wagon train and the great herd of bison in the distance. Vlad was quite impressed with the sketch and he expressed his opinion of it. Acknowledging the gesture, the guide claimed great pleasure in Vlad's approval.

Unsure of how long the conductor would tolerate his absence, Vlad wasted no time in questioning the guide, asking him about the Indians.

"It was not the Devil," said the guide, "but an incarnation of the dead, raised from the spirit world. That's what the Indians claimed to have seen heading west. The Indians often occupy themselves with dancing rituals meant to raise spirits from the dead, so that they will run off the white man." The guide spoke while moving his eyes within a line of focus that must have connected the picture in his lap to the picture of the world laid out before him.

Granting pardon for the confusion about the Devil, the guide expressed some appreciation for the mistake. "The Indians do not believe in a devil," he said, "at least not in the same vein as the one that haunts the Christian mind."

"What do you know about this spirit world that you mentioned?" inquired Vlad. "I'd like to know what the Indians believe about death."

"They believe we ascend to become stars in the night sky," said the guide, continuing to hold his eyes on his work as he spoke. "Unless you die a cowardly death, then you will be taken south to a village of spirits."

Vlad's mind wandered into the village of spirits seeking the significance of its locality. It seemed to him that all mankind's misfortune was most often seen heading south. Then he remembered the tengu. Gensai had once told him about a Buddhist priest who, upon seeing a shooting star, identified it as tengu, or 'heavenly dog'. To see the tengu was to know that war was coming.

"Where will you go?" asked the guide.

The question startled Vlad from his thought. "I beg your pardon," he said.

"When you die," returned the guide, "will you become a star, or go to the village of spirits?"

Vlad did not expect such a question, though it prompted him to take greater interest in the guide. "I suppose I would prefer the village of spirits," answered Vlad, after a moment's consideration.

It appeared to Vlad that the guide did not expect such an answer, for he stopped his work and looked up at Vlad. He seemed to study his eyes as if searching for something. Vlad began to grow curious as to what the guide might find, and just as he thought the man might speak, he heard the voice of the conductor calling from the road.

"Thank you for speaking with me," Vlad said to the guide. The man gave no reply, but continued to study Vlad as he had previously studied the landscape. Vlad turned to walk away leaving the man frozen in his gaze. He wished he had more time to speak with him.

Vlad's thoughts outpaced the horses as they continued across the plains. His mind searched for the face of the Devil, or incarnation of the dead, which had left its spirit world to pursue the living.

He imagined a dark figure riding out ahead of them, commanding wolves and whirlwinds, and turning men against one another. He gazed out of the window and tried to see as the Indians saw. He looked for spirits of the natural forces at work around him. He wondered what the Indians had seen that they identified as their avenger from the dead, and why it was heading west.

He considered the possibility that the Indians had witnessed the effects of his revolver and assumed his coach to be carrying some spirit of the dead. Perhaps the conductor had in fact seen something to the north that day.

His reflections turned, once again, to Ben Ferriday. Perhaps he was known by the Indians, and they had spotted him heading west. There was a man fit to wear the face of death, a vigilante apt to be mistaken for the Devil. He was certainly not averse to assuming the role of the Grim Reaper. Who could know, wondered Vlad, how many people appear to that man as 'underbrush', in need of being cleared away. Perhaps, Ben Ferriday was summoned by an Indian dance to return those lands to 'man's natural habitat'.

Vlad was certain that the Indians would go on dancing in the hope of conjuring death for the White Man, as he was certain that the bones of emigrants would continue to pile up along the road. He would leave it to the Indians to draw a connection between the two affairs.

CHAPTER TEN

AT BENT'S FORT on the Arkansas River, Vlad parted with his companions from the express coach. He would stay with the coach, heading north to the Pike's Peak Express route for Denver, and the ghostly boy and his parents would wait for a coach heading south for Santa Fe.

While his parents were retrieving their luggage from the coach, the boy wandered off, following Vlad toward the fort. High walls built from native stone protected the post, where Bent bartered guns, knives, blankets, and other goods for buffalo hides. The fort sat atop a rocky spur overlooking a bend in the Arkansas River. Apart from processing thousands of hides each year, the fort granted respite to travelers, furnishing supplies and entertainment.

It wasn't until the boy's mother called for her son, that Vlad turned to see the boy following him.

"I want to go with you," said the boy to Vlad.

Briefly, Vlad looked to the boy's parents, then walked over to the boy, hunching down and placing his hands on his knees to look him in the eye. "I can take care of myself," Vlad told him. "Your parents need you to look after them." Vlad stood up and gave the boy a pat on the shoulder. He walked with the boy to meet the boy's father, who was approaching to retrieve him. Vlad was sorry to see the boy go.

Back on the trail, he was astonished to encounter parties heading east, turned back by promises that Pike's Peak was a fool's errand. He tried to imagine the dilemma confronting them after having traveled so far, and wondered if the assertions were true or if they were meant to discourage new treasure hunters from making claims.

Upon reaching Denver, Vlad removed his luggage from the coach, and bid farewell to the conductor and driver.

"Do you know where I might find lodging?" he asked the conductor, before starting off on foot.

"The Denver House," interjected the driver, pointing down the road.

"Don't go there," came a voice over Vlad's shoulder.

He noticed an old man with white hair selling eggs by the road.

When the old peddler saw he had Vlad's attention, he continued. "The Denver House is nothing but an abode of drinking, gambling, brawls, and pistol fights. If I were you, and I was looking for a place to stay, I'd take one of the cabins."

"What cabins?" asked Vlad.

"You just have to look around," said the man, motioning vaguely with his hand. "Many of the cabins are deserted. The occupants either made for mines in the mountains or quit the region altogether, discouraged by what they had to show for their efforts here."

It sounded rather ominous, thought Vlad, a town of abandoned houses. He imagined residents disappearing from their homes, one by one, with nobody knowing where they'd gone. He realized there was no one left to wonder where he was, except Molly, perhaps, or the boy he'd left at Bent's Fort. There was also the crew of the *Magnificent*, at least a few might be curious. He was feeling better about himself, until he remembered Ben Ferriday. He could only hope the old outlaw hunter had given up, if he'd ever truly been looking for Vlad to begin with.

He took a moment to survey the cabins in the distance. Smoke rose from chimneys protruding through roofs of earth-covered saplings. The only proponent of the sun hid blushing behind a grey horizon. He was beginning to feel ill, and at the sound of thunder rolling in ahead of the evening, he decided to continue for the Denver House, despite the old man's advice.

He took care to avoid the main room of the Denver House, which was just as the old peddler had described. Rowdy patrons were busy with drinking and gambling. No one seemed to notice Vlad as he passed through. In the boarding room, he made a bed on the dirt floor next to a man who lay reading a book. Feeling feverish, he lay down and flattened part of his luggage for a pillow. He watched as the wind blew ripples in the flimsy sheeting that served for a roof. Remembering the cabins he saw earlier, his mind returned once again to Shimazu Gensai.

The thatched roofs of Gensai's small village had stood over a field of barley, against a backdrop of green pines and green mountains. Gensai's house was odachi style, open inside, with a row of posts dividing it down the center. It was very modest, outwardly bearing no distinction from the other farmhouses.

"Why do you live here?" Vlad had asked.

"I like it here," said Gensai.

"Will you help me get to Shimoda?" asked Vlad, with faint hope.

There was a pause. "If you can beat me with the sword," said Gensai, finally, "I will help you. If you cannot, you must stay until you can."

"I am not a samurai," he said, and looked at Gensai. "I cannot beat you. You will have to bury me beside my companion."

"We will fight with bamboo swords," said Gensai, "and I will see for myself what you are capable of."

"I cannot beat you," Vlad assured him.

"Then you must stay," replied Gensai.

"Why do you want me to stay?" asked Vlad.

"Because I need your help," answered Gensai.

"Why do you need my help?" pressed Vlad.

"First we fight," insisted Gensai.

For months, the fights were noble silk threads, weaving the days together, like the iron scales of samurai armor. Despite Gensai's fascination at how quickly Vlad advanced under his instruction, Vlad never won a match against him, and despite Vlad's help, the two were never able to accomplish what Gensai had hoped to achieve. Gensai shared an interest in Western culture with the lord of the province, who had acquired a daguerreotype camera and had commissioned his retainers to study it and produce a photograph.

Gensai hoped that with Vlad's help he would be able to master the technology and honor the daimyo with a suitable photograph. Gensai would make trips to bring the camera to Vlad, and they would study it at his house in the countryside. While Vlad had seen such a camera before, he had never used one, and the poor quality of the one the daimyo had acquired made it all the more difficult.

He and Gensai grew so close that Vlad no longer thought of returning to Shimoda, except in the tense moments when he feared he would be forced to go back. Kojiro was an influential samurai at odds with Gensai over Vlad's presence in that place, and threatened to have Vlad expelled from the province by any means necessary. In the end, it was Kojiro, along with those samurai who did not share the daimyo's interest in the West, who destroyed the camera.

Vlad's thought was interrupted by the man beside him, who suddenly rolled off his bed and wormed his way across the floor toward him. He watched, anxiously waiting for the man to stop, but he proceeded until his face was intimately close to Vlad's. He stared at Vlad for a moment, then raised his book and pointed to a spot on the page.

"What's this word?" he asked, with a drunken slur.

Vlad raised his head and squinted to bring the page into focus. He took hold of the book to better orient it in the room's faint light, which loomed near the fireplace on the adjacent wall. "Erytheia," he said, taking care to enunciate the name clearly.

The drunken man's hand had slid from the page, and his index finger hung on his chin. Vlad was surprised to find he had so quickly passed from consciousness. It was as though he had inadvertently cast a spell by uttering the name from the man's book. A mere mortal could not be expected to gaze long into the light of a mythical realm like Erytheia, and especially not when he was drunk. Vlad stood and rolled the man back onto his bed. Reaching for the book, he saw it was a collection of children's stories. He kept the book and lay back down, turning over to the place where the man had left off. The man had been reading 'The Tenth Labor of Heracles' and

Erytheia was the divine hero's destination, the red island of the setting sun.

Sailors will look for the assurance of a red sky at sunset, and Vlad recalled watching a red sunset over Atchison as well as a blood red sky hanging over the Great Plains. He began to envision his journey as the tenth labor of Heracles. He'd been heading west toward Erytheia, though it was not the red-skinned cattle of Geryon that he sought. Vlad was still in the throes of madness, and atonement could wait for the return of his sanity. Perhaps there were no bounds he would not cross to escape the biting chill of death's shadow.

If the West was his island of Erytheia, he must have run aground shortly after Diamond Springs. As he read on, he identified the two lead horsemen that attacked his coach as the two heads of Orthrus, the dog of Erytheia running to confront him, and the third rider as Eurytion the herdsman come to assist Orthrus. He wondered if he should next prepare to face Geryon. He forced the thought from his mind, and focused on his breathing until he fell asleep.

He woke later in the evening feeling as though his health had taken a turn for the worse. His coughing resumed and he felt a fever. His attempts at finding rest were shut out by his aching body, so he decided to try the drinking room, intending on having some whiskey.

The main room was even rowdier than before. Vlad kept his head down, hoping those with something to prove would not mistake his aching eyes as a provocation.

"Did you come for Pike's Peak?" asked the bartender, as he poured Vlad a glass of whiskey.

"No," answered Vlad, "though it appears to have granted a vision of ascent that has captured the entire country."

"Where are you from?" asked the bartender.

"Back East," said Vlad.

"I'm from Oregon," remarked the bartender, as though it were an accomplishment. "Made a mail run from California to Salt Lake City. We were ambushed by Indians. I was the only one that made it. I rode my horse to death and barely reached Salt Lake City on foot. Anyway, that's how I ended up down here."

"Have you spent any time in the mountains?" asked Vlad.

"A little," said the bartender. "A waste of time, though. Why'd you come out here, if you're not looking for gold, you headed to California?"

"I'm looking for a physician by the name of Gordon Newhall," said Vlad. "He came out here to establish an infirmary in the mountains. I don't suppose you've heard anything of the sort?"

"Can't say I have," said the bartender before turning his attention to another patron seeking whiskey.

Vlad took his drink and stood against the wall. In front of him was a group of men gathered around a card table. A man who looked to be the same age as Vlad stumbled over to him.

"You don't look so good," slurred the man.

"You're one to talk," Vlad replied, raising his glass as if to toast.

The man dropped his head, then snapped back up, and gave Vlad a serious glare before forcing a laugh. As he laughed, he slapped Vlad on the chest, taking notice that Vlad was carrying a gun under his lapel. He grabbed the left quarter of Vlad's coat, and pulled it open as Vlad pulled back in an attempt to close it.

"Oh pretty!" the man exaggerated, as Vlad stepped to the right to pull away. "Look Noah!" he called over his shoulder, then reached for Vlad's revolver.

Vlad took hold of his hand and twisted it away from him, forcing the instigator off balance. An older man whom Vlad assumed was Noah turned around from his card table. "Damn it Freddy," he shouted, and grasped the shoulder of Freddy's coat.

At this, Vlad released Freddy's hand. Freddy stumbled backward and then stepped forward, raising a revolver to Vlad's chin. He was astonished at how quickly Freddy had procured the gun. Without hesitation, he pushed Freddy's hand into the air just as the revolver fired, sending a ball through the cloth roof.

As soon as the shot was fired, he pivoted and kicked Freddy in the gut, knocking him backward off his feet. He had his revolver drawn by the time Freddy hit the floor.

"No," shouted the older man, Noah, waving his hands at Vlad.

Vlad saw that Freddy's revolver had been jolted from his grasp by his contact with the floor, so he returned his revolver to its holster. He glanced over at Noah to see him eyeing the revolver. The sight of it seemed to affect Noah in much the same way that it had affected Ben Ferriday. He closed his coat to conceal the gun. Noah's attention was forced back to the floor where Freddy was in need of assistance.

After hitting the floor, Freddy's momentum had carried him into the legs of a man standing at another card table. The man fell backward and landed on top of Freddy. Clearly unhappy about the interruption, the man began delivering blows to Freddy's face until he was stopped by Noah. Noah turned to call another man and demanded that he remove Freddy.

The brawl had held the room's attention for a moment, but everyone quickly returned to their own affairs. By the look of it, the roof was no stranger to gunfire.

Vlad decided that this was an opportunity for his own departure, so he followed the wall around the table to the right, intending to make for the door. As he rounded the table, he was met by Noah.

"Hold on, son," he said. "I'm sorry about that. He's had a little too much to drink. I was hoping you might tell me where you got that revolver."

He looked at Noah, but could not bring himself to answer the question, for his mind was focused on the door.

"Come on now," Noah pleaded, motioning for him to sit. "Let me buy you a drink."

Vlad watched as a larger man, carrying Freddy's revolver in one hand, used his other hand to usher Freddy toward the exit. He decided that sitting for a drink might pose less of a risk than refusing.

He took a seat across from Noah at a small table next to the wall. Noah started to sit, then appearing to remember his offer, corrected himself and headed to the bar. He returned with drinks and handed a glass to Vlad before sitting. He introduced himself as Noah Haggerty and asked for Vlad's name in return. Having given his name, Vlad acknowledged Mr. Haggerty's reply. It was a reply he had become accustomed to receiving, usually an abandoned remark regarding a first encounter with the name D'Agostino.

"I wanted to ask you about your revolver," began Mr. Haggerty, "because I think I've seen it before. Where did you get it?"

"It was given to me as a gift," said Vlad.

Mr. Haggerty examined Vlad for a moment, as if to ascertain the sincerity of his answer. "I know who that revolver belonged to," he said, finally.

"Are you going to tell me that he is looking for it?" Vlad asked.

The question provoked something of a smirk from Mr. Haggerty. "The man I knew died a long time ago," he replied.

"How did you know him?" questioned Vlad.

"I financed some land for him, back in Iowa," answered Mr. Haggerty.

"You were a speculator," Vlad replied.

"That's right," said Mr. Haggerty. "There were a lot of people in Iowa who believed that revolver had a curse on it."

"What do you mean?" asked Vlad.

"They said that the revolver doesn't miss," explained Mr. Haggerty, "and that it doesn't merely kill, but makes a big mess in doing so."

Vlad was taken aback by this, in consideration of his own experience with the revolver. He turned his head to deliberate and studied the dirt floor. He felt an inclination to tell the man about his experience with the gun on the Great Plains, but the whiskey had yet to subdue the throbbing in his head, and he thought to use his words sparingly.

His eyes came into focus on a boot tapping nervously on the floor, and he looked to the table above, at three men fixated on their cards. One of the men had placed his revolver on the table in front of him, and the man with the restless foot sat stroking a coin with his thumb. Wondering if the coin was for luck, Vlad paused on the idea of superstition, and his musing returned him to the company at his own table.

"How did it come to be thought of as a curse?" inquired Vlad.

"There was an attack on the property that I sold to the gun's prior owner," said Mr. Haggerty. "It was Sioux Indians, and the gun was used in defense of the man's children. Allegedly, six shots were all that was required to effect a massacre."

"Sioux Indians?" mumbled Vlad. "What about the man, the gun's prior owner? What happened to him?" He asked this with renewed interest, as his thoughts began to run away with the crazy idea that the gun's prior owner might have been his father.

"He became something of a trouble-maker," answered Mr. Haggerty. "He lost his wife to cholera, and everything seemed to fall apart for him after that."

"Cholera?" asked Vlad. "Might it have been consumption?"

"Perhaps," admitted Mr. Haggerty, dismissing the question. "Regardless, her death proved to be more than her husband could bear. Eventually, he caused trouble with someone he shouldn't have and was shot."

"Someone he shouldn't have?" inquired Vlad.

"Actually," said Noah. "I'm getting things confused. It was the Indians that came back for him, I believe."

He was struck by the awkwardness of Mr. Haggerty's correction, though other curiosities kept him from dwelling on it. "Do you know anything about this engraving?" asked Vlad, holding up the revolver so Mr. Haggerty could examine it.

"I can't say that I do," he answered. "I remember a suggestion that it was a symbol from Eastern Catholicism, although, I also recalled a suggestion that it was of an Egyptian origin."

It was about this time that Vlad heard more gunfire coming from outside the building. The shots were of little distraction to the rest of the patrons focused on their cards and whiskey.

It was not long before the large man, whom Vlad had seen escorting Freddy from the room, returned to speak with Mr. Haggerty.

He overheard the man explaining to Mr. Haggerty that Freddy had begun wildly discharging his revolver in the street and injured a man. Some of the locals had since confiscated his revolver and taken him to a cabin, which was being used as a jail, and their intent was to keep him there for at least the night.

"Why did you give him back his revolver?" Mr. Haggerty questioned the man, though it was more of a charge. The man lowered his head, and Mr. Haggerty stood, appearing ready to depart. When he stood, Vlad stood with him. While the two had been discussing Freddy's predicament, Vlad's mind continued to dart about Mr. Haggerty's story, which made his head ache all the more. He was still trying to determine if the bits of information were coincidence, or perhaps evidence of his father's past. It seemed to him a rather fantastic suspicion, but he needed more information, if for nothing more than to calm his nerves.

The time for questions had come to an end, but Vlad stopped Mr. Haggerty in the hope of posing a final request. "What was the name of the man from your story," he asked, specifying, "the revolver's prior owner?"

"Why don't you come back here in the morning," replied Mr. Haggerty, "and we can resume our conversation." He turned and moved toward the door, then stopped. He looked back at Vlad and then up toward the roof, breathing out a heavy sigh, as though attempting to recall something. "The man's name was Victor Marshak," he said at last. "A Slavic name, I believe. Like Vlad."

It seemed to Vlad that Mr. Haggerty's countenance changed with this last remark. His expression was almost menacing. Perhaps Vlad had detained him too long. It might have troubled him more were it not for the impact of the name Mr. Haggerty had mentioned. It hit Vlad like a blow to his chest, knocking the wind from his lungs. He could not have responded, had he even been able to think of a reply.

Mr. Haggerty positioned a bowler hat on his head, and tipped it to Vlad, signaling his farewell. "Mr. D'Agostino," he said, with a half-grin. "Until tomorrow." He appeared to study Vlad for a moment before disappearing through the door.

Vlad was thankful that Mr. Haggerty had left before observing how long he stared blankly at the wall. He was somewhat consoled by the likelihood that there was no color in his face to begin with. His heart was beating fast and it was the name Victor, rather than the fever, that provoked it. The man shared his father's name, though he knew nothing of the name Marshak.

Once again, he thought of the Daughters of Charity, and the likelihood that they had given him and his sister the name D'Agostino. He wondered if the new name was an effort to spare them from a past tied to another. Had he gone to question Sister Caroline when he'd stopped in St. Louis, she might have been able to answer this question. Perhaps, she would have known whether his name was once Marshak.

He sat in the drinking room for a time, unsure if he should try to catch up with Mr. Haggerty, or attempt to get some rest. Eventually, he staggered back to his bed, while his mind stubbornly returned to the story of Victor Marshak. He did not want to wait for morning to speak with Mr. Haggerty, though he decided he could use the time to think of better questions to ask. Mr. Haggerty might have answers that he could use to fill in the blank pages of his past. Perhaps it would help him to understand how his story should end. He lay in the dark, dreaming up many ideas and circumstances to accompany the details that Mr. Haggerty had given, and when he finally fell asleep, he dreamt of much worse.

He remembered the image of a door and a man's leg stepping through as the door closed behind him. Vlad and his sister were alone, shut in a house in the Iowa Territory. He realized that it was his father who had stepped out, but he was unable to open the door to follow him. He pulled desperately at the door, believing it was his last chance to catch a glimpse of the mysterious figure.

His inability to budge the door led him to the suspicion that something was not right, and his suspicion was subsequently addressed by the onset of an imposing hum that quickly filled the room. The sound began to crush his lungs and sank his heart into his stomach. He realized that the walls were chinked with blood, and the blood began to flow down over the logs.

He turned to see his sister standing on a chair. She had pulled back the sheeting over the window to look outside. He called to her, but she was frozen in her gaze. He looked hard at the image of her standing there, all that was left of a vanishing world, which threatened to leave him abandoned and alone. She had been captured by the heavy sound that steadily grew deeper.

He tried to run to her, to pull her away from the window, but he could barely move. Time itself had seemed to slow down, in danger of stopping completely. He looked to the floor, attempting to witness the source of his impeded steps, though he found nothing, which unexpectedly narrowed his suspicion to the crippling sound of the imposing hum.

When he looked back to the chair by the window, he saw only a large burning candle where his sister had stood. Melting wax flowed down the candle like the blood on the walls, the scourge of mortality. The horror was more than he could bear.

He woke in a sweat. The day's light soaked through the cloth roof. It took all his strength to lift his head, and he let himself fall back into bed. A thought jolted him, as though it were a result of his head hitting his luggage. Mr. Haggerty evoked his recollection of Ben Ferriday, and the possibility occurred to him that Mr. Ferriday may have spent time in Iowa. That might explain Mr. Ferriday's reaction at the sight of his revolver. He would have to ascertain whether Mr. Haggerty was familiar with the name Ben Ferriday.

It was already midday, and Mr. Haggerty was not to be found in the drinking room. Vlad inquired of a clerk as to the whereabouts of the cabin where Freddy was taken after he'd been apprehended. He learned that Freddy had been released to Noah Haggerty, and they had left for Salt Lake City.

"Most people try to avoid Freddy," remarked the clerk.

"It is Mr. Haggerty I need to speak with," replied Vlad.

"Well," began the clerk, "you know where he's going. You shouldn't have any trouble catching a coach to Salt Lake City. It seems everyone is headed the other direction these days. Only the wealthiest people are still heading north, but they're going to Felicity."

"Felicity?" asked Vlad.

"You haven't heard of Felicity?" asked the clerk. "It's a parlor house north of here, on the Cache La Poudre River. Prettiest girls you'll ever see, so I'm told. It's no saloon. You don't go there without money, and lots of it. I've heard talk of parties at Felicity where the madame served caviar and champagne from Paris."

"I don't suppose you have heard anything about an infirmary in the mountains?" asked Vlad, when the clerk had finished. "Or the name Gordon Newhall—Dr Newhall?"

"I don't believe I have," answered the clerk, appearing to give it some thought.

"I was told they are the Never Summer Mountains," said Vlad.

"Never Summer?" replied the clerk. "That's what the Arapaho Indians call the range west of Longs Peak. They say the harsh winters are because of the White Owl." The clerk paused for a grin. "According to an Arapaho myth, the White Owl defeated the Thunder Bird after they challenged each other with their powers. Surely, your doctor didn't go to those mountains."

"How would I reach them," asked Vlad.

"You'd have to head north to Thomson's Creek," said the clerk, "then follow it into the mountains. If you kept to the ridge line, I suppose you'd eventually run into the Never Summer Mountains."

Knowing that he would be unable to rest easy until given another opportunity to question Mr. Haggerty, Vlad decided to resume his journey in spite of his condition. He would have to cross Thomson's Creek on the way, and could decide then whether or not to continue pursuing the past.

Contrary to the clerk's presumption, Salt Lake City was a popular destination that day, and Vlad had to vie for a seat on the coach. After crossing the Platte River and a tedious fording of Clear Creek, the coach pushed on toward the upper route. When the sun finally set over the mountains, they stopped in one of the dry gullies to make camp, hoping to mitigate the cool breeze.

His attempts to rest that night were thwarted by his coughing, and the next day saw his condition worsen. Crossing one of the gullies, the passengers were forced to dismount. Struggling, Vlad reached the top of the high northern bank, but the climb had taken its toll on him. The world was fading quickly as he coughed blood into his handkerchief, and no sooner had he taken his seat on the coach than everything went black.

CHAPTER ELEVEN

THE SOUND OF CREAKING lumber hung like a picture on the dark wall of Vlad's mind. His sense of sleepy eyelids disappeared as quickly as it had come, and he found himself suspended somewhere between a flicker of light and a tranquil darkness that promised refuge from his heavy consciousness. He fumbled to secure a troubling curiosity, the last shade of mindfulness that flickered with the light. He struggled to piece together a familiar anxiety, as though his memories were inconsistent axioms of some mathematical anomaly.

He was back in Gensai's farmhouse, floating on the sea of barley. He sat staring at Gensai's armor, which hung on a rack, appearing as though it were a kneeling samurai warrior poised to jump into action. Its iron scales laced together with braided silk were lacquered bright red, as was the devilish, metal mask, which was fastened to a black, bell-shaped, iron helmet. Riveted to the front of the helmet was a large, u-shaped piece of iron, painted gold and giving the appearance of horns. The inanimate warrior's eyes were frozen open, ever vigilant, waiting with Vlad for the return of its master.

Gensai had left to take back the daimyo's camera. It was late into the afternoon and Gensai had not returned. Fearing the worst, Vlad disguised himself in the armor and set out for the Tōkaidō Road. Kojiro's followers had already been out to the village once to threaten Gensai, making it clear that they would not be satisfied until Vlad was either killed or sent back to Shimoda. Kojiro was the only swordsman that Gensai feared. Gensai shared with Vlad the rumors that Kojiro had studied a school of Chinese Feng Shui, mastering the invisible forces behind all things, and ensuring that he would be unbeatable with the sword. It sounded absurd to Vlad, but he noted that some truth appeared to nourish the roots of most mythologies. In moments of desperation, his mind was willing to entertain even the greatest of improbabilities, and he rode in the hope that Gensai had not met Kojiro on the road.

Vlad did not make it to the Tōkaidō Road before he came upon two of Kojiro's allies approaching the village with Kojiro himself. At the sight of Vlad in Gensai's armor, the first of the riders halted too quickly and fell from his horse. Scrambling to his feet, he led the horse to flee, shouting something about a demon in conjunction with Gensai's name. Kojiro's other ally turned his horse to flee as well. The two had obviously mistaken Vlad for Gensai, though Vlad did not understand their reaction. Only Kojiro and Vlad remained to face one another.

"I watched you die," shouted Kojiro, fitting an arrow in his bow.

The shock and uncertainty of Kojiro's words burned in Vlad like a fuse and exploded in a fury. He charged forward as Kojiro drew and fired. The arrow deflected off the armor that covered his shoulder and before Kojiro could draw another, Vlad ran his horse into Kojiro's and tackled him to the ground.

Vlad landed on top of Kojiro and pushed himself up to punch his adversary in the face. "Where is Gensai?" he demanded.

Kojiro kicked himself free from Vlad and they both scrambled to their feet.

"You are no demon," cried Kojiro, drawing his sword. "You are the foreigner."

Vlad drew his katana and held it as Gensai had taught him.

"Fool," shouted Kojiro, "I cannot be beaten by the sword–"

Vlad did not wait for Kojiro to finish, lunging at him and scooping up from below with his sword. Kojiro brought his sword down on top of Vlad's to parry. Vlad's sword was very old and from a time when the tsuba, designed to protect the hand, was made of stronger metal. Vlad forced the katana across the path of his opponent's sword until it cut through the newer ornamental tsuba and into Kojiro's fingers. Kojiro stumbled backward as though fighting a reflex to drop his sword, and Vlad thrust the blade of his katana into the samurai's torso, running him through.

Vlad kicked Kojiro as he pulled his katana free. Kojiro fell on his back, dropping his sword on his way to the ground.

"Where is Gensai?" Vlad shouted, standing over his enemy. He did not want the answer from Kojiro, but he needed to hear it.

"Dead," breathed Kojiro, wincing, and then he breathed no more.

It was late when Vlad came across the camera. It had been broken and its pieces lay scattered in the road. There was a dog licking the ground ahead and Vlad jumped from his horse to scare it away. Kneeling by the damp blot of dark earth still discernable in the fading light, he began to claw at the dry ground, raking the dirt to cover what he believed was the blood of his friend. He didn't know if he was acting rationally, he knew only that he must do something.

Hiding behind Gensai's mask, Vlad made his way safely to Shimoda, treading a road soaked with his friend's blood. Without Gensai, there was no place for him in the Land of the Rising Sun.

CHAPTER TWELVE

VLAD FELT a wet cloth on his forehead, and he opened his eyes to see a beautiful young woman standing over him. She urged him to drink, so he did, and thanked her for the water. "Where am I?" he asked.

"You're at Felicity," she explained, "the parlor house of Madame LaGrande. This is the doorman's room."

"I was on a coach heading for Salt Lake City," stammered Vlad, trying to make sense of his surroundings.

"You were brought here to see the doctor," offered the young lady. "He said you needed rest."

"You have a doctor?" asked Vlad.

The young woman explained that theirs was a small mining town, and there was no resident doctor. "You are lucky to have caught him," she added.

"Is he still here?" asked Vlad. "What is his name?"

"His name is Dr Allen Olford," she answered, with a look of suspicion, "but I'm afraid he has already left."

"Where is the coach?" asked Vlad, though he was sure he knew the answer.

"They did not stay," replied the young woman.

"And my luggage?" Vlad asked, with greater concern.

"Here," said the young woman, pointing to the floor near the foot of the bed.

"The doorman's room," mumbled Vlad, after a pause. "Where is the doorman?" he asked, surveying the empty room.

"He left town after receiving threats from Noah Haggerty," replied the young woman.

"Is Mr. Haggerty here?" asked Vlad, sitting up. He was taken aback by the mention of the name.

"No," she replied. "He would never set foot in this house."

"Do you know him?" Vlad questioned with excitement. "Is he in town?"

"Everyone around here knows Noah Haggerty," she replied. "He is most often at the land office. What do you want with him?" Her furrowed brow indicated disapproval of Vlad's interest in the man.

"I need to speak with him." Vlad replied, throwing off his covers.

The young woman placed her hand on his shoulder and persuaded him to lie back down. "I'll take you to his office once you have rested," she assured him.

Vlad could not argue with her touch. "How long will the madame permit me to occupy the room?" he asked.

"It is difficult to know with Madame LaGrande," she replied. "The madame would likely prefer the room to be available for the next doorman she hires, but you don't need to worry about that tonight."

Vlad turned his head to examine the room. There was a small table situated beside the bed as a nightstand, and an old chest of drawers sat against the wall. On the floor he saw one end of his luggage protruding from behind the foot of his bed. He looked to the ceiling where narrow boards were fitted tightly for decking atop dark heavy beams. It reminded him of the view from his hammock beneath the deck of the *Magnificent*.

"I might be able to work for her," suggested Vlad, "for a while, perhaps."

"As a doorman?" asked the young woman in surprise. "I don't think so. You don't look like a doorman."

Vlad was not sure if he liked her reply. "Are you one of the madame's girls?" he asked, and did not wait for her answer. "You don't look like a shady lady."

At this, the young woman rose to leave. "You have a fever," she retorted, and she closed the door behind her, leaving Vlad to rest in his bed.

Later that night, he sat up and wiped the sweat from his brow. His ears were ringing, and he could hear the sound of a piano and the bustle of a crowd muffled beneath the floor. Outside the room, he stood in a hallway atop a set of stairs, which he followed down to another hallway. The hallway at the foot of the stairs opened on the left into the parlor and led on the right to the back of the house.

The sounds of the parlor were still muffled in his ears. Disoriented, he stepped slowly through the doorway into the room and stood observing the spectacle as though it were a dream. He would not have expected to observe such luxury in a remote mining town. The room was furnished with every requisite for enjoyment. The walls were decorated with oil paintings. The floor was covered by an elegant arrangement of plush furniture and costly carpets.

A man with a cane crossed in front of him, and Vlad turned to watch him make his way from the bar to take a seat beside the woman who had tended to him earlier. The man wore a black double-breasted frock coat and carried his cane, a fine adornment carved from ebony with an engraved silver ferrule. He sat with the woman on a loveseat that hugged the wall to the right of the hall doorway. The woman intercepted Vlad's inspecting gaze, and her eyes assured him that he'd been caught examining her mauve haute couture dress.

Vlad heard a commotion behind him and he turned back around to face the room as a man burst through the front door with a young woman, whom he shoved to the floor. The sight of the young woman hitting the floor seemed to jolt several of the patrons. The man carrying the cane stood with an expression of disgust. An older man standing at the bar, near the door, took a step toward the intruder, and Vlad realized he too had taken a step toward the man.

"Whoa, Abbott," said the intruder to the older man near the bar. "The sheriff's outside and he asked me to tell Madame LaGrande that, if he ever catches Dana snooping around town again, with a gun," the man paused to hold up a shotgun, "he'll have her hanged for attempted murder."

Abbott tilted his head and looked out the door as Dana began scooting away from her assailant.

"Jacob," Abbott addressed the man as though he were correcting an adolescent, "I don't see the sheriff out there."

Jacob started to turn around but stopped as though making a conscious adjustment. "He was out there," said Jacob. "He's the one that told me to bring Dana in here."

"Well," said Abbott, "you've done that, so I suppose you can be on your way now. I'll take that shotgun. It belongs to the madame." Abbot motioned for Jacob to hand over the gun.

By this time, Dana was back on her feet and standing behind Abbott.

"Maybe I'm not ready to leave, Abbott," said Jacob.

"Why don't you give me that shotgun," said Abbott, taking a step closer to the man.

"On second thought," said Jacob, throwing the shotgun behind the bar. "I'll leave, and I'll take what I came with." He drew a revolver as he spoke and pointed it at Abbott, shoving him to the ground with his off hand.

Pulling away as Jacob reached for her, Dana scampered to take cover behind Vlad and the man with the cane.

"Jacob," said Vlad.

Jacob stopped to look Vlad over. "Do I know you?" he asked with a disdain that suggested his question was also a threat.

"It would appear that you are not welcome here," remarked Vlad, peering into Jacob's eyes as he spoke.

"Are you going to throw me out, pretty boy?" taunted Jacob. As Jacob raised his revolver to escalate his intimidation, Vlad reached to grasp just below the ferrule of the cane, pulling it from the trembling hand of the man at his side. Just as Jacob had his aim, the dark ebony of the opulent walking stick struck him just above the wrist. His forearm collapsed under the weight of the blow.

Jacob's agonizing cry silenced the parlor, and before his revolver hit the floor, Vlad delivered another blow to Jacob's thigh. He toppled over his impaired leg, clutching his deadened forearm with his off hand. The force of his fall whipped his head against the hard wooden floor, and he rolled onto his back, swallowing enough air to bellow another distressful howl. By the time Vlad stood up with Jacob's revolver, Abbott had retrieved the shotgun and was showing Jacob the open end of the barrel.

Vlad handed the cane back to its owner, who inspected it while watching Vlad remove the cylinder from Jacob's revolver. Abbott ordered Jacob back on his feet, and watched Jacob struggle with his two good limbs.

On his feet, he hobbled, turning himself to face Vlad, who was dumping powder from the cylinder of Jacob's gun into an empty glass. "You damn devil," shouted Jacob. "I remember you. You were at the Denver House. You're that bastard that was stupid enough to mess with Fast Freddy. Well guess who's back in town?" Jacob paused, appearing to observe the effects of his dramatic revelation. With a look of dissatisfaction he proceeded with renewed emphasis. "You're a dead man," he said. "You'd better believe I'll be back here with Freddy in the morning."

"Do you believe you're going somewhere?" Vlad replied, noting the fear in Jacob's eyes, before turning to Abbott. "Where's the sheriff?"

"The sheriff isn't going to do anything about this," Abbott declared. "Isn't that right, Jacob?"

"Why are you asking me, old man?" Jacob snarled.

"Play dumb if you want to," returned Abbott. "It suits you, anyway. There may be no justice done, but I'm betting this isn't what the sheriff had in mind, if it was him that sent you in here." Abbott addressed Vlad, whose expression begged for an explanation. "Half this town knows that Jacob here, and the rest of The Untainted take their orders from the sheriff."

"The Untainted?" Vlad questioned.

"That's the name of their gang," explained Abbott. His nerve appeared to waver as his eyes shifted between Jacob and the shotgun in his hands.

"I'm not looking for trouble, Jacob," said Vlad, placing the cylinder back in the revolver and handing the gun to Jacob.

"Well you found it, pretty boy," threatened Jacob, pointing the useless revolver at Vlad. He left his threat to hang in the air as he stormed out of the parlor, slamming the door behind him.

"Why are they called the Untainted?" Vlad asked Abbott, disturbing the silence of the parlor.

"Apparently," said Abbott, "they take issue with brothel entertainment, among other things. Jacob's not one of their exemplary members."

Vlad watched Abbott place the shotgun on the bar, and noted his diverted gaze as he focused on something in the hallway. He turned around to see Dana exiting a room across from the stairs. With Jacob out of the picture, Vlad was free to devote his attention to her appearance. She brushed her disheveled hair away from her face, and he could see her pale skin was flush around her cheeks. Aside from her black hair, she reminded him of Molly, though he suspected the influence of a defiant spirit. She dawdled in the hallway until the bustle of the parlor regained its prior pitch, then she approached with a message for Vlad. "The madame would like to see you in her office."

CHAPTER THIRTEEN

MADAME LAGRANDE sat behind a decoratively carved mahogany desk. Situated in the middle of her office, the desk was a bold fixture squared off to respect transactions that might sooner take place beneath it. In front of the desk sat an upholstered mahogany armchair, a solid-looking piece made to support the heavy desires that weighed down the hearts of Felicity's wealthier patrons.

To the right, against the wall, candelabras lined the top of a chest of drawers. Ornate curtains were draped around a window to the left of the desk, and in the corner nearest the window stood another work of carved mahogany in shelves that stepped up the wall, leading various silver trinkets toward a particular height of luxury. The room's grandeur warned visitors of the price for felicity, an expensive word that was more than a name for the establishment. In that place it was an incantation.

Two large paintings of remote landscapes hung on the wall behind the desk, where Madame LaGrande sat wearing a black dress. Vlad had heard of the timeless beauty of French women. If she was fifty, the madame had reached her age gracefully. Her hair was dark, and pulled back to reveal an attractive quality in the features of her face. Perhaps, it was the confidence in her eyes.

"Close the door," said the madame, without any hint of an accent. Her words fractured the room, like a bolt of lightning splitting through the scenic landscapes of the paintings. "Just what do you think you are doing?" she questioned him, sternly.

"What do you mean?" asked Vlad. "That man was after Dana."

"What is she to you?" snapped the madame. "Who are you?"

"My name is Vlad," was the reply.

"You look like hell," she said. "You were brought here on your deathbed. On your way to Salt Lake City, is that correct?"

"Yes," answered Vlad.

"Then, I suppose you'll be on your way?" asked the madame.

"I think I may stay a while," answered Vlad.

"Do you have a death wish?" asked the madame, and when Vlad did not reply, she continued. "That man was a member of The Untainted."

"I was not aware of this gang," explained Vlad.

"Is that so?" asked the madame. "Because I heard Jacob mention an incident involving you and Fast Freddy down in Denver."

"I was only defending myself in Denver," he replied, though he was bemused and begged her for an explanation. "*Fast* Freddy?" He placed a special emphasis on the word 'fast'. Recalling how quickly Freddy had drawn his revolver, it was not the name that surprised him, but the extent of its recognition.

"The truth is," confessed the madame, "I could use someone like you. Perhaps you're a bully trap. You appear to know how to handle yourself."

"I could use a place to stay," replied Vlad.

"The room upstairs is for the doorman," said the madame, "but you cannot be the doorman." She stood turning to the corner. With her free hand she reached to grasp the back of her neck, and held her posture as if mulling something over.

Vlad thought to ask for an explanation, but decided to wait.

"It's too risky," said the madame, after a moment. "I cannot be seen as employing you. Not as you've gone and made yourself a target for The Untainted. However, as everyone suspects the sheriff to be the head of The Untainted, no one would imagine that I would call on the sheriff if someone, such as yourself, simply refused to vacate the room."

Vlad stood in silence contemplating the madame's suggestion. It had seemed a reasonable proposition when the idea of working as the doorman had been his, but confronted with the madame's proposal, he began to waver. He wondered what kind of trouble loomed over Felicity, that the madame would assume such risks to keep him there. "And as long as I stay," he said, "I suppose you will expect me to keep an eye on the parlor, in the evenings."

"And if Fast Freddy does show up looking for you," said the madame, "I expect you will have the sense to take matters outside, into the street."

"Of course," answered Vlad, astounded that the madame did not consider him more trouble than he was worth. "Is there anything else?"

"Yes," replied the madame. "Stay away from my girls. You may leave the door open on your way out."

Back in the parlor, Vlad spotted Abbott by the door. As he neared the bar, Abbott looked up and spoke first. "I've been thinking about what happened here tonight," he began. "It's unsettling. I'm not sure what I'm going to do, but you should leave town as fast as you can."

"I believe I heard Jacob call you Abbott," said Vlad.

"That's right," returned Abbott.

"I'm Vlad. It's a pleasure to meet you."

Abbott nodded, and reached for his whiskey.

"What makes a man like Freddy so dangerous?" asked Vlad.

Abbott took a drink. "Men come out West knowing how to handle a gun," he began. "Maybe they've served in a militia. Maybe they've even been in a duel, but there's no formality to a gunfight out here. I'm sure you know how to handle a gun, but that isn't going to do you much good against someone like Freddy. He's going to make sure he gets close, and then all that matters is who draws their gun the fastest, and there's no one faster than Freddy."

Vlad watched Abbott take another drink of whiskey. He looked at the whiskey glass after Abbott had set it back on the bar and continued to examine it until he sensed Abbott eyeing him. Looking up, he noticed a portrait on the wall behind Abbott. "Is that Dana?" he asked, and as he turned to point out the portrait, he noticed someone whom he assumed was another of Felicity's girls standing over his shoulder.

"Ha," chuckled the girl. "A portrait of Dana! That'll be the day."

"Do you see no resemblance?" asked Vlad, after taking note of the girl.

"I wouldn't concern myself with Dana, if I were you," replied the girl. "She's spoken for." She pressed her index finger into her lips, which formed a devious smile. "But don't tell anyone I told you."

Vlad turned to Abbott, who turned back to the bar. "I thought I chased away her greatest admirer," he said, playfully exaggerating a glance around the parlor. "Nice fellow," he quipped, looking up at her, which prompted her to roll her eyes and walk away.

"Who was she?" asked Vlad, turning back to Abbott.

"Liz," replied Abbott. "She's a fiery one."

Vlad gave an acknowledging smile. "I suppose you are the doorman?" he asked,

"Why do you suppose that?" returned Abbott.

"You are sitting by the door," said Vlad, "and you tried to stop Jacob."

"Well, I'm not the doorman," insisted Abbott.

"Perhaps you should be," suggested Vlad, maintaining his poker face.

"Perhaps, you should tell that to the madame," replied Abbott. "Every time one of her bouncers runs off, I make her a new offer."

"You must know how to handle a place like this," said Vlad, examining Abbott, who stared at the liquor cabinet behind the bar as though he were no longer aware of Vlad's presence. Vlad glanced at the bottles of various shapes and sizes strewn across the cabinet, wondering how long they might hold Abbott's attention.

Vlad's patience appeared to be too great a distraction for the man, as Abbott fumbled to take a drink of whiskey, nearly spilling it on himself. "Well, this is the spot a doorman ought to be," he said, wiping his mouth and turning back to Vlad. "The only reason to stand anywhere else would be to talk to one of the patrons, and a doorman will be talking to the patrons, if he knows what he's doing." He stopped to look Vlad in the eye, and questioned him. "You ever work as a doorman before?"

"I have not," answered Vlad.

"Well," continued Abbott, "a good doorman doesn't have to throw anyone out, because he talks to everyone. If a patron is informed regarding proper behavior, like an actor groomed for a role in a play, then he will be inclined to play the part. The challenge is keeping the wrong sort from entering the parlor in the first place. From where we're standing, we may observe those intent on entering the parlor, and turn back the ones who know better."

"Like Jacob," conjectured Vlad. "How do you recognize the wrong sort?" he asked.

"It is the responsibility of everyone who works for Madame LaGrande to ensure that her patrons are enjoying themselves," answered Abbott. "Anyone who appears as though they might cause a problem should not be permitted to enter the parlor. Look around. These people didn't come from the mines. They're either here profiting from the treasure hunters, or they are simply not from here. Rich bastards come from great distances to visit the house of Madame LaGrande."

"Why are you here?" asked Vlad.

Abbott looked away as if to turn the page and prevent Vlad from reading any further. "I like the whiskey," muttered Abbott. There was a pause before he spoke again. "I've never seen anything like that before."

"Like what?" asked Vlad.

"What you did to Jacob Parnell," answered Abbott. "Maybe you should be the doorman," he added, chuckling.

"Perhaps, I'll stick around and keep an eye on you," quipped Vlad.

"If you value your life," returned Abbott, "you'll do as I suggested and get out of town while you can."

Vlad smiled and headed back to the hall where he found the stairs. Upstairs, there were sounds that refused to be held behind closed doors, and he wondered if it was the sound of genuine pleasure or merely show business. Inattentively, he opened his door, still minding the erogenous cries that echoed in the hall. Standing in the doorway, he was startled at the sight of Dana. She stood up from his bed and met him at the door. Stepping forward she grabbed the lapels of his coat. "You need to leave," she said. "You have to get away from here before they come back." The look on her face expressed confusion as to why Vlad did not respond. Her eyes moved to his lips and followed them as they moved slowly to meet hers.

Vlad looked into her eyes as he pulled away. "I'm not leaving."

Dana appeared to study the look in his eyes, and after a long pause, she rose to the tips of her toes to kiss him once more, but only for a moment. Pulling away, and letting go of his coat, she ran her fingers across his arm, then stepped out of the room and disappeared down the hall.

CHAPTER FOURTEEN

IT WAS AFTER NOON when Vlad ambled back into the parlor. According to regulation, the shades were drawn to keep the darkness within from spilling out onto the street and clouding the pure light presumed to shine in the eyes of passers-by. The bustle of the prior night had receded with the shadows before dawn, leaving a profound quiet to fill the parlor.

His gaze was fixed on the far wall where a large painting hung between the windows. It was the portrait he'd spotted the night before, of a young woman whose long black hair hung in sharp contrast to her porcelain-white skin. With his eyes fixed on her, he moved closer. If the portrait were to let out a sigh, he would have felt the young woman's breath on his face.

"I see you've met Saint Dorothy," came a voice from behind him.

He turned around to spot a fairy-like creature standing in the doorway. It wasn't until she spoke that he realized he had traced the curve of her hip beneath her chemise, which was just long enough to touch her bare thighs.

"Bella," she spoke while moving toward the fireplace.

Vlad recognized her as the young woman who had cared for him the night before. "Bella?" he questioned her, his confusion made apparent by the expression on his face.

"That's my name," she explained. "And you're Vlad, is that right?"

"That's right," he replied, grinning at himself.

"So, you're still in the doorman's room," remarked Bella.

"That's right," said Vlad.

"Are you the new doorman?" asked Bella.

"Do I look like a doorman?" answered Vlad.

Bella smiled.

"The madame refused to employ me as such," Vlad explained.

"It's a shame," spoke Bella. "I saw what you did to Jacob." When Vlad made no comment, she continued. "I saw you talking to Abbott," she said, looking away as though embarrassed by her admission.

"Yes," said Vlad. "What is his story? It seems he would make a decent doorman."

"He would like that, I'm sure," explained Bella. "I think he would like to stay here. All the girls think he is in love with the madame. Gerty said he followed her here from New Orleans. She said he is an old client."

"I see," said Vlad.

"I think the madame is annoyed by him," Bella continued, "but she won't ask him to leave. He is always helping out around here."

Vlad smiled and then turned back to the painting. From the corner of his eye he could see Bella looking at the canvas with him.

"The girl in the painting," said Bella, after a moment, "her eyes follow you wherever you go."

Vlad kept his eyes on the portrait. "Yes," he remarked, "I noticed that last night." He looked back to Bella, sitting by the fire, her eyes still on the painting. "You called her Saint Dorothy?"

"She reminds me of a painting of Saint Dorothy that I remember from when I was a child," said Bella. "Whenever I look at it, I hear my mother telling me that God is always watching." Bella grew silent, appearing lost in her stare. "I hate that painting," she said, finally.

Vlad watched as Bella dropped her eyes and pushed her hands across her closed thighs to rest them on her bare knees.

"Why are you here?" asked Vlad. "At Felicity."

"Where else can a girl earn such a living?" answered Bella. "Or wear such beautiful clothing as we do? Why do you think we're not allowed in town at this hour? All the other women in town are jealous. They're out and about their business, afraid that their husbands might find themselves bewitched at the sight of one of us walking down the street."

"Perhaps, they're right," said Vlad, smiling.

Bella look down, again, and folded her hands around her knees.

"How closely have you looked at this painting?" he asked.

Bella gave him a puzzled look, and he continued. "If you look closely," he said, "you will see that what you thought were watchful eyes are but the careful brush strokes of human creativity."

She continued to stare at Vlad as though she were looking out at the sea, then she rose to join him in front of the portrait. After a time of peering into the eyes of Saint Dorothy, she turned to offer Vlad a smile. He returned the smile and spoke to question her. "I thought the portrait was of Dana," he began. "Do you know where she is?"

"She's…" Bella started, then stopped herself, directing her eyes back to the painting.

"Has she gone into town?" Vlad attempted to draw Bella back from her distraction.

"No," she said, speaking to the floor in front of her feet.

"Oh, right," said Vlad, watching her wiggle her big toe. "You said you are not permitted in town at this hour. I don't suppose you will be showing me to the land office, then."

"It's not hard to find," said Bella. "It's just before the general store, if you're heading west on the main street." She looked up at Vlad, then back to the hallway. "Gerty made turkey and rice," she exclaimed. "You should have some before you go. It's very good."

He followed her into the kitchen, chewing on curiosity, and contemplating the authority of hunger. Light poured through the curtains, and, outside, he knew his eyes could wander freely without risk of bumping into Bella's partially covered curves. Perhaps Dana would join them.

CHAPTER FIFTEEN

FELICITY STOOD NEAR the end of a short street on the outskirts of town. The street climbed out of a sharp bend, leveling to continue past the parlor house, and was barred from going much further by trees, which climbed a small hill to the north. Houses stretched out from the hill like the arms of the Sphinx, trapping Vlad in the street.

The dark log walls of Felicity blended with those of the other houses that filed down the street and wrapped around the bend to the east. The house on the corner hid all but the rooftops of the buildings below, which lined the town's main street, cutting west through the trees. He walked up the street into the treeline, hoping for a better view, and his attention was drawn southwest over the housetops.

A sea of dying leaves danced around the town, burnished red by the afternoon sun. At a distance to be regarded with suspicion, mountains climbed over mountains rising toward the immense snow-capped peaks, which held the sky aloft over the West. Drifting near the highest point was a single cloud or waft of snow, brushed from Longs Peak as it cut into the dizzy sky.

Upon reaching the main street, he observed more of the dark logs characteristic of the town's houses, which also formed the facades of the hotels, saloons, and stables, facing off across the street in booming competition. The sound of wagon wheels and shouting drivers bounced down the street, trapped beneath the arcade of covered platforms. He looked ahead to the edge of town where the road disappeared into a dusty haze of trees, masking the mountainous barrier that encroached from the west.

He found the land office situated next to the general store, as Bella had described. Inside, he was met by an older man standing behind a counter ensconced before a doorway leading to the back.

"Good afternoon," said Vlad, returning the man's greeting.

"Can I help you, son?" asked the man. Salty skin and wiry grey hair provoked a second look before Vlad could decide that the man behind the counter was not Mr. Haggerty.

"I'm looking for Noah Haggerty," said Vlad.

"Noah's out of town," replied the man. "Is there something I can help you with?" The old man's speech indicated impatience.

"I spoke with Noah in Denver a few days ago," said Vlad. "I was hoping for an opportunity to speak with him again." Vlad's admission was met with silence. He held his gaze in what felt like a staring contest, though it was only a moment before the silence bested the old man.

"Look," the old man said, "I already told you he's out of town. I handle most of Noah's affairs. What is it you're wanting to talk to him about?"

It was far from the friendliest of invitations, but Vlad was driven by his own impatience and a desire for answers. "It isn't business related," he began. "He was telling me about a man named Victor Marshak."

The old man's eyes widened, and he straightened himself into his tallest posture. Taking his hands off the counter, he took a step sideways and lowered his voice. "Why do you want to know about Victor Marshak?"

Though puzzling, the old man's reaction seemed to demonstrate an acquaintance, and Vlad saw this as an opportunity. He pulled back his left lapel to expose his revolver. "I don't suppose you are familiar with this?" he asked, pointing to the engraving.

The old man squinted at the revolver, then his eyes grew even wider than before, and he nearly fell against the counter. He jumped back, pulled a sawed-off shotgun from beneath the counter, and steadied it on Vlad.

Vlad raised his hands, trying to calm the man. "Whoa."

The old man's voice was now a stern growl. "Who are you?"

"My name is Vlad D'Agostino," he said, calmly, "I have questions, that is all."

"What questions?" The old man's eyes looked as though they might pop.

Vlad was hesitant to tend to his desire for answers at the expense of caution. It would be dangerous to turn his back on the urgency of understanding the situation he had just walked into, but, for the moment, any question seemed as good as the next. "To begin with," he said, slowly, "I was hoping to find out who killed Victor Marshak. Must you point that at me?"

"You came to the wrong place for answers, son," growled the man. "You don't have any business here, so I'll advise you to back out of here."

Vlad's relief to know that the man did not intend on firing the shotgun fell short of compensating for his disappointment. The window of opportunity was closing, and he could almost see what he had come for. "This is a misunderstanding," he said. "If I could speak with Noah—"

"Noah's not here," shouted the man. "How many times do I have to tell you that?"

"When will he—"

"When he gets back," the man interrupted, "I'll tell him you're looking for him. Now, you need to back out of here."

"Alright," agreed Vlad, keeping his hands in the air as he backed toward the door. "Do you know who killed Victor Marshak?" he asked in desperation.

"Indians," barked the old man.

"Noah said it was someone Victor shouldn't have messed with," said Vlad, playing a hunch.

"Ben Ferriday," mumbled the old man, as though questioning himself.

"Pardon?" asked Vlad, desperately.

The old man stepped out from behind the counter and moved toward Vlad. Vlad stepped back through the door onto the platform. The old man stood on the other side of the doorway pushing his gun into Vlad's chest. He slowly dropped his hand from the forestock of the shotgun and reached for the door. His eyes rose slightly before snapping back to Vlad. "Ben Ferriday," spoke the man, sternly, before slamming the door in Vlad's face.

The name circled around Vlad like a wall of flames burning up the outside air. Breathing heavily through his nose, he continued to chase the name as his feet led him back down the street. He reached the east end of town before realizing he had passed the turn to Felicity, then stood for a moment watching his shadow stretch to the East.

Doubling back, he made his way up the street to Felicity. He continued past the parlor house to the foot of the hill and stepped into the trees, turning to face another red sunset. Looking toward Erytheia, he struggled to cast the role of Geryon in his story. Who would prove to be the fearsome giant that he must confront, Death or Ben Ferriday? Perhaps, the two were one and the same. His eyes narrowed as he considered the weight of his revolver against his chest. If the gun really was cursed, he assured himself, Ben would need more than Geryon's three shields for protection.

By the time he returned to Felicity, he found that the parlor had already come to life. He was greeted by Abbott as he stepped through the door.

"What are you doing here?" asked Abbott.

"I live here," replied Vlad, forcing a smile to lighten his mood, "remember?" He settled in next to Abbott at the bar.

"What kind of arrangement do you have with the madame?" asked Abbott.

"Oh, don't worry, Abbott," said Vlad, "I won't be around much longer."

Abbott looked at Vlad as if trying to discern his meaning. Vlad acknowledged the ambiguity. If it weren't for his disease, or The Untainted, the suggestion might have born its more common implication.

"I think I'll push on for Salt Lake City," explained Vlad. "I suppose I can trust you to look after this place."

Abbott smiled and so did Vlad.

"Why do you think the madame refuses your offer to work as the doorman?" asked Vlad.

"Oh," said Abbott, "I suppose she'd prefer it if I left town as well."

"Why do you suppose that?" asked Vlad.

"She and I go back before this place," said Abbott. "I followed her out here thinking she might eventually want something more than silver. She's got this damned aversion to anything that might weigh her down, any fixtures that aren't made from precious metals."

"Does a woman like the madame ever decide to settle down?" asked Vlad. "You may turn to silver yourself before that day ever comes."

"We'll see," was Abbott's reply. "That woman will be attractive at any age. You'll never hear her complain about how old she looks. She says that aging well is the true measure of beauty."

Vlad turned to step away from the bar and nearly collided with Dana as she stood and spun into his path. Not bothering to look up, she stepped away from him and headed toward the doorway to the hall.

"Dana," Vlad called after her.

She stopped and spun around to offer him a foul glare, then turned back around and disappeared into the hallway and up the stairs. He looked to the man with whom Dana had been sitting. The man did not wait for Vlad's eyes to meet his, turning his head to Liz who sat on the arm of the loveseat. Her hand was rested on his shoulder and her eyes intercepted Vlad's gaze. She wore a sinister smile that seemed to mock him, and she looked down to the man before Vlad's eyes could question her. He wondered if it was he, or Dana, that was the source of Liz's avocation.

He followed Dana, catching up to her at the top of the stairs. "Is everything alright?" he asked her.

Scoffing, she turned to him with the same foul glare as before. "No. Everything's not alright, Vlad."

"What is it?" asked Vlad.

"Gerty said you went looking for Noah Haggerty today," answered Dana, continuing down the hall.

"Yes," said Vlad, becoming somewhat frustrated. "What of it?"

Dana stood facing her door. "What do you want with Mr. Haggerty?" she asked, after a pause.

Vlad found it difficult to answer such a bold question. "I think he may have known my father," he said bluntly.

Dana huffed, pushed herself into her room, and closed the door behind her.

Dumbfounded, Vlad rushed into his room and slammed the door, confused by the anger that compelled him to act so rashly. Embarrassed, he remained in his room for a time, before heading back down to the parlor.

CHAPTER SIXTEEN

NIGHT FELL with the rain, and morning played the same steady cadence on the roof of Felicity. Vlad felt the room rock like the hull of the *Magnificent*. He lay in bed, breathing deeply to calm himself, and began to analyze the images and emotions that lingered from a dream.

He was in the hull of the *Magnificent*, and a dark figure that he knew to be Death had bound his hands. As Death led him to the deck, he passed by his shipmates, each offering an apologetic glance before cowering back to witness Vlad's impending doom. Death was stubbornly persistent and pulled him along steadily. Reaching the gunwale there was no hesitation as Death pulled him over into the dark water below. It was the cold that roused him.

The sound of a gunshot rang out, as if to signal the end of his contemplation. Snapped from his trance, he wondered if there had been an actual gunshot, or if it was a ricochet from the past, a resonance that had woken him previously, like the one from his memory of the Missouri steamboat, sounding out over the northern shore of the Big Muddy.

His thought was interrupted by the sound of more gunfire and a commotion in the hall. A woman's shout preceded rapping on the door. "Vlad," she cried, "Fast Freddy is in the street demanding that you present yourself. Jacob Parnell is with him, firing his revolver at Felicity."

"I'm coming," Vlad shouted, as he rolled out of bed.

Outside the door, the girls had gathered in the hall above the stairs. When Vlad stepped out of the room, they turned their eyes as though ashamed of all that a mere glance might offer. They seemed to be the same apologetic glances from his dream. Only Dana's eyes followed him, appearing to watch with something like curiosity. Nearing the bottom of the stairs, he looked back to see some of the girls peeking over the railing above, to watch him disappear through the open door of fate.

In the parlor, Madame LaGrande peered through the curtains into the street. At the sound of Vlad's footsteps behind her, she spun around, letting go of the curtains. She hurried over to him, whispering under her breath. "You knew this was coming," she told him.

"I suppose," answered Vlad. "May I have a glass of whiskey."

The madame stared at Vlad until her stern demeanor changed to one of understanding. He expressed no concern with what she might have thought she understood. It was enough that she was moving around the bar to retrieve his drink. He placed his hand on the bar in front of the glass, waiting in anticipation as she poured. From the corner of his eye he saw Dana appear in the hall. He stepped toward the door and pulled the glass from the counter as soon as the madame had lifted the bottle. He raised the glass to smell the whiskey as he proceeded to the exit.

The rain outside had slowed to a drizzle. He stood in the doorway and called to the two men who appeared to be scanning the upper windows of Felicity. "Freddy," he shouted, "we've been cheated of a proper introduction. Why don't you come in and have a drink?" He finished by holding up the glass to show the whiskey.

Freddy glared through the mist with a focus that appeared settled on interpreting the invitation as an insult. "Get out here you damned devil," he demanded, "and I'll give you a proper introduction."

Jacob backed away from Freddy as Vlad stepped into the street. Vlad shifted the glass of whiskey to his left hand and stepped away from Felicity, maintaining his distance from Freddy. He took a drink of the whiskey, keeping his eyes fixed on Freddy's right hand.

Freddy glared at the glass as though attempting to set the whiskey on fire with the force of his will. His face wrinkled, and he stretched his fingers as if prepared to lift himself from the ground by his belt.

His revolver hung on his right hip, but his left hand mirrored the right, as though neither functioned independently of the other.

No sooner had Vlad lowered the glass than Freddy's hand slapped his waist. Immediately, Vlad flung the glass into the air toward Freddy. Freddy's eyes followed the glass as he wildly fired a shot into the rooftops across the street. By the time he removed himself from the path of the whiskey glass, Vlad was on one knee taking aim with his revolver. The percussion of Vlad's shot thundered through the street, chasing away the resonant blast of Freddy's gun, like the ripples of a second stone dropped into water. Vlad's ears rang with a reverberation that seemed to slow time, and he watched as though still in a dream while the scene advanced like ink spots spreading across a blank page.

The ball from his revolver tore through the air and then tore through Freddy, ripping his throat out through the side of his neck. Surprised again by the accuracy of his shot, he readied himself to face the consequences of firing his cursed revolver.

Standing behind Freddy, Jacob was doused in a bucket of blood. He clapped his hands over his eyes and let out a shrill cry. After wiping the blood from his eyes, he held out his hands, still wailing, and looked over to his fallen comrade who was flopping on the ground like a fish out of water, drowning in his own blood, only able to proffer a gargle for a cry.

Looking up at Vlad, who had risen to his feet, Jacob turned to run. Nearly tripping from his start, he buried his shoulder into the wall of Felicity, which spun him face first into the dark log siding. Pushing himself away from the wall, he staggered trying not to step on his chin, and when he finally regained his balance, he scampered down the street with his chafed face in one hand. After a moment, he disappeared around the corner, and the street lay still as the cold rain washed away its iniquities.

Vlad stood in the stillness, unable to look away from the tragic picture. He expected the bloody scene to burn red hot upon his skin, dry his mouth, and make his heart beat faster, but he was calm. What stirred him was curiosity, bewilderment in his ability to coolly stand before the horror of it. When he finally looked away, it was not because he had seen enough. He had chased a thought and lost it in the vexing apprehension of advancing scrutiny, inquisitive eyes encroaching upon the street.

Returning to Felicity, Vlad was met by the madame, and directed to use the back door. Inside, he ascended the stairs methodically, undressed, and fell into bed.

CHAPTER SEVENTEEN

VLAD MIGHT HAVE EXPECTED Felicity to be in an uproar that evening, and it was, but not the kind of uproar he could have foreseen. On his way to the parlor, he heard a voice coming from the hall at the bottom of the stairs.

"Do you think this is wise?" questioned the voice. "You don't want to provoke the sheriff."

"Don't worry," came the reply, which was clearly the madame's. "He's not going to risk confirming his affiliation with The Untainted."

Stepping into the hall, Vlad gave the madame a start, which drew a laugh from Abbott, who was standing in front of her.

"There he is," the madame cried, "my hero. Look," she motioned for him to follow her.

Vlad stepped out of the hall and stopped to observe the parlor as he had yet to see it, packed wall to wall with patrons lifting their spirits with glasses of champagne. The madame retrieved a glass from behind the bar and held it up for him to observe.

"It didn't break," she exclaimed. "It must have landed in the mud. It's the whiskey glass that bested Fast Freddy."

Vlad returned a half-smile of acknowledgment and then looked at the floor. The madame walked to the back of the bar and placed the glass on a shelf. Abbott stepped up to Vlad's shoulder. "It seems your heroics, or madness, is cause for celebration." He held his whiskey with both hands and his eyes appeared to trace the craggy surface of faces that careened like a flock of birds, to and fro between the walls of Felicity's parlor. "I thought you were leaving for Salt Lake City," added Abbott.

"I've not made up my mind on that," replied Vlad.

"All the familiar faces are here," declared Abbott, after a pause.

"Along with everyone else, it would appear," said Vlad, smiling at Abbott as he spoke.

"There's Dirch Brewer," exclaimed Abbott, "who all the women blush for. They might blush for you too, if you had some color in your skin. Story goes that Dirch ran off with a beautiful young dancer he found in Weston, Missouri a few years back. When she discovered he was married, she killed herself. Rumor has it, you can see her still, if you catch Dirch in the right light after midnight, for it's her shadow he casts in the witching hours."

Vlad raised his eyebrows and pursed his lips into a grin for a response.

"See those two there?" continued Abbott. "The man on the left is the proprietor of the Northern Exchange

Saloon, and the Grand Hotel was established by the man on the right. Ah, the man talking to them now is a curious fellow. His name is Hugo Dunning. Apparently, he used to be a magician, but made his fortune later from gambling. His wife is a real beauty. She often makes herself available at the Northern Exchange. It's no secret to Hugo's wife that he frequents Felicity. It's assumed that their marriage is more of a business arrangement."

Abbott paused for a drink, and Vlad looked out over the room. Was this the sort of place he might expect to find Ben Ferriday? He tried to recall the sound of the man's voice, which had seemed so familiar, but the thought was drowned out by the noise of the parlor. Perhaps it was the noise that blurred his attempts to recall the features of Mr. Ferriday's face, though he had no doubt he would recognize him if his face were to appear in the crowd before him. Perhaps Mr. Ferriday was hiding in Hugo Dunning's hat he thought, suddenly embarrassed to be smiling, as he would be unable to answer for it.

"You've seen Rob Vance at the bar, I'm sure," Abbott began again, ignoring Vlad's smile and gesturing with a nod. "He was heading west when he lost his wife at a river crossing. He spends his nights at the bar until he's liquored up enough to convince himself that one of Felicity's girls is the reincarnation of his wife. The girls have all lost interest in the routine.

Some nights the madame coerces one of them to oblige the poor soul, and other nights she keeps the drinks coming until he's unable to order another. That's when we drag him into the kitchen to make room at the bar for someone else. We'll be dragging Chuck Wilcox to the kitchen later for sure. He never fails to fall asleep in one of the chairs once he's had a few drinks. One morning, Rob woke up under the kitchen table with his arm around Chuck after we'd dragged the both of them to the kitchen." Abbott laughed at the memory.

"Is that the end of your gossip, old man?" Vlad quipped.

Abbott appeared to ignore the comment. "Hal Stillman over there is one of the new regulars," he continued. "He's a famous architect. He designed some marvel of a government building back East, I can't remember which city." Abbott paused again, as though attempting to answer the riddle he had just presented to himself.

Not waiting for Abbott to resume his stories, Vlad allowed the shifting swarm of patrons to guide him to the bar where he was intercepted by a crowd eager for *his* story.

A man with a handlebar mustache spoke up to address Vlad. "Tell us, how is it that you came to reside here at Felicity?"

Vlad examined the mustache. "I can't think of anything worth mentioning about it," he replied. "I set out from Denver on a stagecoach, and I ended up here."

"Denver?" questioned an old man behind Abbott, who had followed Vlad to the bar. The man leaned back to get a look at Vlad. "A lot of folks here from Denver recently, all running from the Devil. Is that why you're here?"

"I'm just passing through," Vlad insisted, disoriented by the mention of a devil. That strange corridor through the Great Plains had led him to a place where devils roamed freely and the setting sun always burned red, reflecting the blood spilled by cursed revolvers. Perhaps, his revolver belonged to the Devil, and the Devil was looking to retrieve it. Maybe, Ben Ferriday was the Denver Devil.

"What's this about the Devil?" questioned the man with the mustache, and everyone looked to the man at the bar as he began his reply.

"A man named Ted Knowles saw the Devil down in Denver, and I heard that if you had seen the look on Ted's face when he told the story, you'd have had no choice but to believe him."

"So everyone's leaving Denver because this man claimed to see the Devil," interrupted the man with the mustache. "And where is Ted Knowles?"

"Dead," answered the man at the bar. "Some say the Devil killed him. Others say he killed himself, 'cause he couldn't stand the thought of the Devil coming back for him."

"Did he say what the Devil looked like?" asked Vlad, drawing a condescending glance from the man with the mustache.

"Come on," the mustache interjected, "you're not really listening to old Rusty Guts, here? If the alleged Mr. Knowles saw anything, it was probably an Indian."

"He said his face was black and disfigured," answered the old man. "He had glowing red eyes and sharp horns, rounded back like a goat's. There was a rumor around town that other people had seen it, too."

"That's enough ghost stories, gentlemen," interrupted the madame, having suddenly appeared behind the counter, "this party is for the living. Now, who wants another drink?"

"On the house?" someone shouted.

"Don't be ridiculous," returned the madame. "Nothing at Felicity is 'on the house'."

"What about the champagne?" pressed another.

"You can all thank Vlad for that," replied the madame.

Vlad stepped away from the bar intent on locating a change of scenery. As he scanned the room he saw Dirch Brewer, the good-looking gentleman that Abbott had pointed out earlier. He noticed something behind the man, floating in the margins of his view, an effeminate form lingering near the wall. He brought the woman into focus, first to verify that she was not the shadow of the young dancer from Missouri, and second, to verify that she was not Dana.

"So, what are you going to do if the rest of The Untainted show up for revenge?" shouted a voice.

Glancing back, Vlad found the man with the mustache eyeing him expectantly. In spite of the man's intention, it was not Vlad who answered.

"If they want Vlad," announced Abbott, "they'll have to get past me first."

Vlad looked to Abbott, and in the brief moment when Abbott returned a glance, Vlad nodded to offer his gratitude.

He heard someone jesting about Abbott putting himself in danger of standing for a cause, but Vlad had already turned to explore the parlor, content to leave Abbott's answer as the final word on the matter.

From the corner of his eye, he saw the back door open. His view was obstructed by guests preoccupied with one another, but he thought he recognized Dana stepping out. Something protruded from her shawl, and he was convinced that it was a blade. He worked his way to the hall, and hurried up the stairs to his room.

A lamp was lit and left to sit upon the chest of drawers. His bag lay open on the floor, and the sheath of his katana lay empty beside it. He started to reach for it, but walked over to the window. It was dark, but he was able to make out a figure moving between the houses on the other side of the street. Dashing back to his luggage, he knelt and began rummaging through it. He found the wakizashi, and as he pulled it from the bag, Gensai's samurai mask came out with it, unraveled from the cloth in which it had been bound.

He stared at the mask for a moment, surprised by the same placidity with which he had stood before Freddy's dead body. He did not understand how, but he had forgotten the mask. As he looked at it, he thought of the Denver Devil of which the old man had spoken. Lifting the mask from the floor, he was reminded of Gensai, and he understood that it had not been fear that had driven him to take it, a shameful desire to save himself. He had taken the mask, and worn it, in order to help his friend. He stood tucking the mask and wakizashi under his coat, then made for the back door.

The air outside was cold, but as he stepped into the darkness around the corner, it was difficult to see his breath. Across the street, he made his way between the houses where he had last observed the figure he believed to be Dana. Stopping at the back corner of one of the houses, he placed his hand on the cool logs and peered down the corridor that ran behind the row of buildings lining the street. Although he could not see far down the passageway, the sound of voices assured him someone was there. As he rounded the corner, he recognized one of the voices, which had risen to a shout. It was the voice of Jacob Parnell.

Vlad took the mask from his coat and pulled it over his head. Attempting to stay light on his feet, he moved quickly down the corridor until he saw Jacob around the corner of one of the buildings. Jacob's back was to Vlad, and he stood in the light from a nearby window, holding Vlad's katana over his head. He was threatening to bring the blade down upon Dana, who lay on the ground at his feet. Another man stood opposite Jacob, positioned to prevent Dana from escaping down the alley.

"I said, where did you get this?" shouted Jacob.

"From the Devil," said Dana, defiantly, appearing to have caught sight of Vlad approaching from behind Jacob.

"That's the last smart remark you're ever gonna make," said Jacob, raising the sword higher. He made a hissing sound as he sucked the air in through his teeth.

Lunging forward, Vlad grabbed the hilt of the katana just above Jacob's hands as he drove the blade of his wakizashi through Jacob's torso. Leaving the wakizashi in place, Vlad stepped forward, now in command of the katana. Spinning around, he swung the sword, severing Jacob's head from his body.

Dana screamed and the man blocking the alley screamed with her. Looking through his mask, Vlad leaped over Dana toward Jacob's accomplice. The man fell backward, tripping on his heels, then turned and scampered on all fours before regaining his footing to flee the alley. After the man had disappeared into the darkness, Vlad walked back to Jacob's body to retrieve the wakizashi.

"What are you doing?" he asked Dana, as he cleaned the blood from his swords with Jacob's coat.

Dana rose cautiously to her feet, keeping her eyes on Vlad. She began backing down the alley and then turned to run. Vlad followed her to the end of the alley, then stopped to watch her cross the street to Felicity. He removed the mask and stowed it as best he could with the swords beneath his coat.

Back at Felicity, Vlad returned his things to his room before heading to the parlor. He helped Abbott carry Chuck Wilcox into the kitchen, where they laid him against the wall behind the table. Rob Vance had escaped before the inevitability of a shared fate could snare him. Attempting to direct his thoughts away from the dark alley, he wondered if Rob had managed to locate his late wife hiding behind the willing eyes of one of Felicity's girls.

"Abbott," said Vlad, following him back to the bar. "Do you remember the other night, when Jacob brought Dana into the parlor?"

"How in the world could I forget that?" replied Abbott.

"He said that Dana was snooping around with a gun," remarked Vlad.

"That's right," said Abbott.

"Do you know what she was doing?" asked Vlad.

Abbott shook his head as he stepped up to the bar. "She's got a death wish, that one," said Abbott. "She was going after the sheriff." Abbott appeared to take note of Vlad's confusion. "It's a long story."

"I'd like to hear it," said Vlad.

Abbott picked up a glass of whiskey. "Dana's family was on their way here when their party was attacked by Indians," he began. "Several were killed, including some of the emigrants. In the end, the Indians made off with Dana. She was seventeen at the time. After months of failed efforts to free her, a deal was struck through negotiations. It was over a year ago when her father, Bob, agreed to pay a ransom. It took all the money he had to get his daughter back, and without money, Bob approached Noah Haggerty to discuss the terms of a loan. Noah offered him financing on some land just outside of town, and Bob took it. As with all the land here, much work is needed to make it profitable. Now Bob's deep in debt and exposed to continual harassment from The Untainted. It wasn't long ago, they burned down his barn. Dana's brother died trying to save their horses. Dana blames the sheriff, and she's been looking for revenge ever since."

"Why is she at Felicity," asked Vlad, "if she has family here?"

"The madame comes across as a hard woman," said Abbott, "but she's got a soft spot for these girls. She believes she's giving them a better life. If they weren't here, they might be on the street, or down at the saloons. Anyway, I think she's found a way to help Bob Sobol, without him or anyone else knowing about it. I think that's why Dana is here."

"I cannot imagine her father being able to tolerate it," remarked Vlad.

"There's not much he can do," said Abbott. "He's got an obligation to Noah Haggerty, and showing up here at Felicity has proven to provoke The Untainted. Most people think that's why they burned down his barn. It happened right after he showed up here asking for Dana. The Untainted's hatred for Felicity is no secret, they would just as soon see this place burned to the ground. They don't seem to have any issues with the saloons, though. Sad thing is, there was a man who sold a mining claim near here for a small fortune. He offered to settle Bob's debts in return for Dana's hand, but he was sufficiently harassed by Jacob and The Untainted so that he fled in fear of his life."

"How do you make sense of that?" asked Vlad.

"I don't," said Abbott. "I'm just telling you what I know. Most men won't have anything to do with Dana after they find out she's been tainted by Indians."

"Tainted?" asked Vlad.

"Well," said Abbott, "you can imagine what the Indians did to the girl while they held her captive."

Vlad distracted himself by focusing on the sounds of the parlor, until his mind settled back on Jacob, but the same thought that had previously distressed him began to ease into a kind of relief. He looked up to the ceiling, studying again the skillful woodwork. The thought of lawless men clashed with the neat lines that ran between the beams.

He caught himself looking to the ceiling many more times that night, until the parlor cleared, and Dirch Brewer was seen fleeing the tragic gloom of his deceased love, whose shadow bathed in the last wave of darkness before twilight. All but Gerty, the parlourmaid, slipped beneath the covers of their beds to hide, like vampires, from the rising sun.

In his room, a faint light painted the floor beneath the curtains and revealed that Dana was asleep in his bed. He was happy to see her. He hoped never to see her reduced to a mere shadow, even if it was his shadow. If his shadow was to be hijacked, he'd just as soon see it stolen altogether. Although he liked the idea of Dana wearing his shadow after he was gone, he did not wish the burden on her. Perhaps only after midnight, he thought, smiling to himself.

He removed his coat and trousers and lay down next to Dana. He watched her lift her eyelids under the heavy weight of sleep. Holding Vlad's gaze, she placed her hand on his chest, and slipped her fingers into his shirt, between the buttons. He reached to place his hand on the small of her back and pulled her closer. Dana turned her head, interrupting a brief kiss.

"There is something about me that you should know," she said.

"It doesn't matter," said Vlad, running his fingers into her hair and guiding her lips back to his.

They kissed behind a faint light too dim to separate their shadows. As time went on, the curtains masked the morning as twilight, and cloaked Vlad in dreamless sleep.

CHAPTER EIGHTEEN

WHEN THE CURTAINS could no longer hold back the day's light, Vlad found himself shivering and alone. He had kicked one of his feet free from the covers and slept that way until the chill roused him. He brought his knees into his chest and pulled the covers over his head. Dana was gone, but he could still smell her, sweet and earthy, like rain, or the ichor that ran in the veins of the gods. Warmed by his thoughts, he drifted back to sleep.

By the time he rolled out of bed, it was midafternoon. Standing in front of the window, he looked across the street to the place where he had watched Dana disappear into the night. The events of the prior night hid in isolated shadows, scattered like a dream cut short by the light of day. Perhaps he would have to answer for what he had done. Maybe he had stayed too long in bed, or shed the heavy weight of burden when he threw off the blanket, for a sprightly emotion filled him and fueled the desire to spur this fight he had started.

He washed and went down to the parlor to find Gerty, from whom he was able to procure a plate of bread, cheese, and a sugar cake. When he had finished, he thanked her and stepped outside.

Walking down the street, he arched his back and rolled his shoulders forward to free himself from the stiffness that still clung to him from sleep. He felt the rumble from a train of thought, and kept his gaze on Longs Peak while he walked, suspecting that at any moment the vibrant aspects that suspended his senses would come crashing down in an avalanche of inspiration.

His pace slowed as he struggled to take in the novelty of the brilliant day. Every color appeared in distinct contrast. The town was still new to him, but even the trees appeared as oddities previously unknown, or as something he had forgotten.

He thought briefly of Freddy, imagining his adversary's tragic life flashing before his eyes as he had lain dying in the mud. The events of Freddy's life painted by the brush strokes of memories had finally emerged, a complete picture. Vlad had come to the West to buy more time, but he began to wonder if more time was truly what he desired. It might be the limited amount of time he had that made his life worth living.

He walked along the south side of the town's main street to take in the warmth of the sun. The sounds of the street's traffic flittered around his ears like a mosquito trying to distract him from his focus on the mountains to the west. He stood for a moment in front of the land office until he became aware that he had stopped.

He walked through the door slowly, preparing to place his hands in the air, but the salty old man who had previously held him at gunpoint was not at the counter. No one was at the counter, though as he took a step forward, he saw someone approaching from the hallway. He stood watching, until a figure appeared behind the counter to greet him. His coat and collar indicated that he was a minister of the Methodist Church.

"Hello Reverend," said Vlad.

"Are you looking for someone?" asked the minister.

"Noah Haggerty," answered Vlad.

"I'm sorry," returned the minister, "but he is not here. I'm afraid no one is at the moment. Zach has gone to Salt Lake City, and was kind enough to let me borrow the office. We're going to build a church at the end of the street, if you've not heard."

Vlad showed a smile in acknowledgment of the minister's enthusiasm. He assumed Zach must be the man who had sent him away after his prior visit to the office, without giving him a chance. "Did Zach say when Noah would be returning?" he asked.

"I'm afraid not," answered the minister, continuing to speak with an apologetic voice. "I'm sorry, son, I cannot help noticing your appearance. You'll forgive me for asking, but is it consumption?"

The minister wore the same look that Vlad had become accustomed to receiving. "Do not fret Reverend," said Vlad. "It should not be troubling me for much longer."

"If you are not speaking from sarcasm," began the minister, "then I admire your placidity. I assume you have made a confession?"

"A confession," Vlad muttered to himself. "May I borrow a pen and paper?" he asked the minister.

"I don't suppose Noah would mind," replied the minister.

"I was thinking on the way here about the placidity that you mentioned," remarked Vlad, as the reverend fulfilled his request. "I would like to write, before I lose the impression." He examined the newer fountain pen the minister had given him. It was elegantly crafted with a silver nib and a band of silver embroidery around the front of a black barrel. It seemed a little extravagant for the piece of old manila stock he'd been given to write on.

"Impression," puzzled the minister, "I thought you were going to make a confession."

"I suppose I could confess many things," admitted Vlad, "but I do not know what good could come of it. I would prefer to write something that might be of value to someone else."

It appeared to take the minister some time to acknowledge Vlad's response. "I suppose I mistook you," he remarked vaguely.

Vlad did not respond, but focused instead on the paper he had received from the minister.

The minister appeared to grow impatient. "What of eternal suffering?" he asked, finally. "Have you no concern for your soul?"

"Eternal suffering," Vlad murmured inquisitively, trying to write. Some time passed in silence. "Where is the contrast in eternal life?" he asked aloud.

"I don't understand your question," answered the minister.

"Consider your appreciation of the day," Vlad began, still focused on his writing. "The value is a product of an understanding that the sun will set, and the day will end. If the day did not end, your appreciation of it would eventually be scorched by never-ending sunlight. You would soon become like a bison, stampeding across the plains compelled only by animal passions. Were it not for the hunger in your great, bison stomach, even the grass would lose its flavor. What need would you have of even these passions in eternal life? Do our lives not retain value only insofar as they are limited? You say there is eternal life, and if I say there is nothing, I believe we are essentially saying the same thing."

"You're the Devil," exclaimed the minister.

"I've been called that more than once recently," remarked Vlad. "Fast Freddy was the last, I believe," he heard himself say.

"I know who you are," the minister shouted. "You're the pistoleer from Felicity."

"You've heard of me?" inquired Vlad.

"You're not the Devil," returned the minister. "You're a fool," he said, shaking his finger at Vlad. "You have no idea what you've been drawn into. Why, you've unwittingly damaged the interests of that wretched woman in whose brothel you've taken up residence."

"What makes you say that?" asked Vlad.

"You killed Freddy Mangan," replied the minister. "He was the most imposing member of The Untainted, a gang that obeys the wishes of Madame LaGrande."

Vlad lifted his pen from the paper and sat up straight, taken aback by the minister's suggestion. He looked over his writing for a moment, then set his pen back to work on the page. "I've heard of The Untainted," he said, "but I am certain that Madame LaGrande's only interest with the gang is in its demise. I suppose next you will suggest that she keeps me only in the hope of contracting my disease."

"I do not know why she keeps you," the minister declared sternly, "but I can assure you that she drives The Untainted to do damage to the assets of the good Mr.

Haggerty. He is the only man in this town possessing enough decency to see it rid of her whores and–"

"I believe you are confused," Vlad interrupted, looking up from his paper. "The Untainted cannot be at odds with Mr. Haggerty. I have witnessed, first-hand, Noah Haggerty's association with Fast Freddy. Noah himself bailed Freddy out of jail down in Denver, and that was after his mingling with Freddy at the Denver House. Why would a man behave this way toward his enemy?"

"Since I have known Noah," argued the minister, "I have witnessed his generosity on many occasions. Why, he is practically the sole source of funding for our new church. I know nothing of any affiliation with Fast Freddy, but I can say that even Judas was permitted to dine with the Lord. As for your madame, why do you suppose she is in the habit of transferring funds to the sheriff? We all know that The Untainted are his men."

"I know nothing of it," replied Vlad, returning to finish his writing.

"Perhaps you should ask her," suggested the minister.

"Perhaps I will," remarked Vlad, as he returned the pen. "Thank you, Reverend."

Vlad stepped out onto the covered platform of the land office, and the minister stepped out behind him. They both stood looking at a crowd that had gathered in the street, around the open bed of a wagon.

CHAPTER NINETEEN

A SHORT WALK brought Vlad to the Grand Hotel. He stood to examine the facade, while attempting to recall the face of its proprietor, whom he had just met the night before.

Turning toward the sound of running footsteps, he had only a moment to recognized Dana before she slipped her arm around his. They spun together to face two men, halting their pursuit.

"You," shouted one of them. "She's not supposed to be here."

Vlad studied the men for a time before making a reply. "Are any of us, really?" he asked, receiving a queer look.

"She's wanted for questioning," stated the other of Dana's pursuers.

"What sort of questioning?" asked Vlad.

"Regarding the murder of Jacob Parnell," replied the man.

"I see," said Vlad. "I suppose that's who you've got in the back of that wagon over there."

"That's right."

"How do you know he didn't kill himself?" asked Vlad, with a straight face. "I had but two encounters with the man, and he seemed dreadfully unhappy on both occasions."

"He was found decapitated," answered one of the men, appearing to lose patience with their conversation.

"Is that so?" Vlad intoned a question. "And how do you suppose a lady might manage such a feat?"

"She's no lady," shouted the man.

"Perhaps not," said Vlad, looking at Dana defiantly, "and she's not supposed to be here, you'll recall. I believe I'll see her back to Felicity. You may call on her there."

"You may not have done it, you witch," the man continued shouting after Dana, as his partner headed for the saloon, "but you're going to answer for the devil that did this."

With his back turned to the man, Vlad allowed himself to grin at the man's remark. "What are you up to?" he puzzled, looking down at Dana.

"What are *you* up to?" she replied. "Why did you kill Jacob? I'm glad you did, but I have good reason to be content in his death. What reason do you have?"

"I was making an impression," answered Vlad, surprised by Dana's challenge.

"An impression?" repeated Dana, blushing.

"Yes," said Vlad.

"You can't be serious," said Dana.

"I was speaking of–I meant an impression on The Untainted," said Vlad, embarrassed by the confusion. "Perhaps, they will be less eager to threaten you now."

"Why did you come to this town?" asked Dana, after they had walked a moment in silence.

"I came to find someone," said Vlad, "a doctor."

"What doctor?" asked Dana.

"It doesn't matter," said Vlad. "I don't think it was actually him I hoped to find. I think I was looking more for something like redemption." He paused to look at Dana, who appeared to be studying him. "Have you heard the story of Heracles?" he asked.

"Of course," Dana answered, wiggling her nose.

"My mind often wanders late at night as I lie attempting to rest," began Vlad. "When I was in Denver, I thought about the tenth labor of Heracles. Heracles was tasked with twelve labors, as a penance, for the tenth he was ordered to retrieve cattle from the monster Geryon at the end of the world, on the island of Erytheia. It was also known as the red isle of the setting sun." He paused again to observe Dana, who appeared to be listening intently. "I began to think of all the red sunsets I have seen, and I felt that I too was heading toward the end of the world to face a monster. In Denver, I entertained a fantasy that, once I had found what I was looking for, I might see a different sunset, as though I had passed beyond the red island. Now, I feel as if my labor is complete, and what I thought to be a monster is actually the greatest of sunsets. It sounds rather silly, I suppose."

"It sounds rather poetic," said Dana.

Vlad laughed.

"Why is that funny?" asked Dana.

"I suppose it is inspiration burning me up from within," said Vlad.

"What?" asked Dana.

"It's nothing," said Vlad. "You remind me of someone I met in Manhattan."

As he turned to continue on his way, he caught a glimpse of a man in black coming down the street from the land office. He counted two others following closely behind.

Taking in enough to recognize the white collar, and desiring no further confrontation with the minister, nor with the men behind him, Vlad turned away from them, and began again down the street, escorting Dana and quickening his pace. After a moment, they crossed the street. Vlad used the opportunity to take advantage of his periphery. Behind him, all three men were crossing the street as well.

"What is it?" asked Dana, looking back with him.

"We need to get back to Felicity," said Vlad, as they turned at the street to the parlor house and began the uphill jaunt. After they rounded the first bend, Vlad made out his pursuers turning onto the street behind him. Quickly rounding the last bend, he and Dana ducked into the alley between the two houses that stood before Felicity.

"What are we doing here?" asked Dana.

Vlad raised a finger to his lips to implore her silence, and watched from the shadows as the man in black strolled by looking up at the house tops, as though he were in pursuit of nothing more than the scenery.

He was not the minister. He was a priest. His appearance tempted Vlad to consider whether he was dreaming. The sight of the priest was a riddle that he was unable to attend to, for he had been spotted by one of the two men who followed. He stood paralyzed, stung by life's brutish wit, staring at the origin of some unsung proverb. The intuition that he was being pursued was justified by the image of this man who had now stepped into the alley. It was Ben Ferriday. Vlad grasped his right lapel and began to back away down the alley, keeping Dana behind him.

"It *is* you," cried Mr. Ferriday, raising a hand to plead for patience. "I've been hoping to catch up to you. I want to ask you about that revolver that you were carrying on the train."

A fat man behind Mr. Ferriday pushed by, rushing at Vlad, while attempting to draw a revolver from the opposite side of his waist.

"No," shouted Mr. Ferriday, reaching in vain for the fat man's shoulder.

Vlad stepped forward to meet the man. Releasing his hold on his lapel, he swung the back of his hand into the side of the fat man's neck and followed through, swimming by as the man fell to the ground. Vlad's momentum brought him face to face with Mr. Ferriday. He grabbed Mr. Ferriday by the collar and drove him to the ground. With his free hand he drew his revolver and shoved it into Mr. Ferriday's face.

"This revolver?" he questioned hotly. "The revolver that belonged to Victor Marshak, the man you killed?"

Mr. Ferriday's eyes lit in obvious rage, and he buried his fist into the side of Vlad's head. Disoriented, Vlad quickly stood and took a step back, keeping his gun on Mr. Ferriday while he shook off the blow. He was ready to pull the trigger, if Mr. Ferriday should reach for a gun.

"Don't you ever say that again," shouted Mr. Ferriday, losing control of his voice. "Victor was my friend." He breathed heavily for a moment while the two stared at one another. "There's no doubt," said Mr. Ferriday, rolling slowly onto all fours and pushing himself back on his feet, "I've attracted too much attention walking the streets in the open— shouting, and such. One of Noah's men is sure to have spotted me. I can't stay here." He glanced to the fat man still lying on the ground. "Is he alright?"

There was no doubting the sincerity in Mr. Ferriday's eyes when he spoke of Victor Marshak. Vlad kept his focused on Mr. Ferriday, and knelt to feel the fat man's pulse. "I think he's alright," he said as he picked up the unconscious man's revolver.

Noticing Dana behind Vlad, Mr. Ferriday tipped his hat. "Ma'am," he said. "My apologies for the all the fuss."

Dana appeared to study Mr. Ferriday, but gave no reply.

"On the train," said Vlad, "when you saw my revolver, I watched you reach for your gun."

"I was attempting to retrieve my spectacles," argued Mr. Ferriday. "Since the train, I have been considering the possibility that you are Victor's boy. Are you?"

"I have only recently learned of the name Marshak," answered Vlad. "I have been wondering the same as you."

"If you would like to talk about Victor," replied Mr. Ferriday, "meet me at Zander's Ferry. I'll be there until morning."

"Zander's Ferry?" inquired Vlad.

"The river crossing," Mr. Ferriday clarified. "Head west out of town, it's not far after the road turns north. You can come with me now, if you like."

"What about him?" asked Vlad, gesturing to the man on the ground.

"He's not with me," Mr. Ferriday assured him. "I was asking him about Fast Freddy Mangan, when I spotted you. I couldn't convince him to stop following me. He said he and Freddy were part of a gang called The Untainted, and that you killed Freddy, but we can talk about all that later. Are you coming?"

"I'll come later," Vlad promised, though unsure of his sincerity. He kept his gun in hand until Mr. Ferriday returned to the street, and watched from the alley, with Dana, until the old outlaw hunter disappeared around the bend. After Vlad laid the unconscious man's gun on the ground, he and Dana started again for Felicity.

"You don't truly intend on going to Zander's Ferry?" asked Dana.

"Do you think it's a trap?" asked Vlad

"I don't think you should find out," she replied. "What do you suppose he meant by 'Noah's men'?"

"I too found that curious," answered Vlad, "perhaps I should go find out."

Dana gave no reply, but stared blankly ahead, appearing lost in thought.

Vlad noted that Mr. Ferriday's apparent paranoia was ironic, given his own recurring anxiety from their encounter on the Hannibal and St. Joseph Railroad. It appeared Mr. Ferriday was not quite as cool headed as he portrayed himself in his stories.

CHAPTER TWENTY

BACK AT FELICITY, Vlad found Abbott stacking wood by the fireplace in the parlor. He approached to greet him, as Dana disappeared into the hall.

"Where have you been?" asked Abbott.

Vlad nearly stumbled into the deep pit of his imagination in deciding how to answer. Something in the back of his mind challenged his judgment as to whether he really knew where he had been. In the end, it was the land office that he mentioned. "I wonder if I may borrow your horse this evening, Abbott?" he asked.

"I don't see why not," answered Abbot. "Where do you intend on going, if I may ask?"

"Do you know of Zander's Ferry?" asked Vlad.

"Of course," announced Abbott. "What about it?"

"I need to meet someone there," Vlad told him.

He watched as Abbott shoveled ashes from beneath an iron grate that stretched across the base of the fireplace. It was a large fireplace encased in fashionable stone. An ornately carved mantel and similarly styled legs framed the stone, making the fireplace a fitting anchor for the extravagance of the parlor.

"Do you want me to go with you?" asked Abbott.

"Do you have another horse?" replied Vlad.

"Well, no," stammered Abbot, "but—"

"You should stay and watch the parlor," Vlad suggested. "I won't be long."

"You better keep an eye out for The Untainted," Abbott warned him.

Vlad closed his eyes as he nodded. In the hall, he was prepared to climb the stairs when he noticed the madame sitting at her desk in her office. Remembering his conversation with the minister, he gave a knock on the open door. "Excuse me, Madame," he said.

"What is it?" spoke the madame.

"I was hoping you might tell me what you know of The Untainted," said Vlad.

The madame evaluated him for a moment. "Why do you ask?" she questioned him, finally.

"I'm interested to know who is behind their actions," confessed Vlad.

"I thought you understood that it is the sheriff's gang," said the madame.

"Yes, but what are the sheriff's motives?" Vlad pressed. "And is he even the highest power at play?"

She evaluated him once more. "I don't think the answers to those questions are going to be of any use to you," she began. "There is a complex dynamic behind what goes on in this town, and further involvement on your part may prove difficult to manage."

"You don't need to worry about me, Madame," said Vlad, with a sarcastic grin.

"It isn't you I am worried about," answered the madame. "I have a responsibility to these girls."

"Is that why you pay the sheriff?" Vlad challenged her.

"Yes," answered the madame curtly, "I pay fines to the sheriff. Is it beyond your insight to expect that a corrupt man might take advantage of a business such as mine?"

"I suppose not," answered Vlad. The madame's answer merely confirmed his suspicion, and he regretted that he had troubled her with the question. "Please excuse me, Madame."

Upstairs, he found Dana standing by the window in his room. He glanced out of the window as he walked over and placed his hand on her hip. "It is quite a view," he whispered, "even in the twilight."

"It is the best view in the house," returned Dana. "There's Longs Peak. You can see it from Ellen's room, too, but only if you hold your head out of the window."

"Ellen?" asked Vlad.

"The madame," answered Dana, with a look of embarrassment.

Vlad looked out the window to Longs Peak, as it faded into a blackened sky. "On the other side of that mountain lies the place I came out West to find," he said.

"What is out there?" asked Dana.

"A longer life, perhaps," answered Vlad.

"You should go," said Dana.

"I think I prefer a short life," said Vlad, still looking out the window. "One filled with every season. I can only imagine the desolation of a place with no summer. What's the point of living if everything is frozen?"

"You don't mean it," said Dana. "You're only being poetic, again."

"Were you watching the sunset earlier?" asked Vlad, after an awkward pause.

"Yes," she admitted.

"What color was it?" he asked.

"Don't go, Vlad," she said.

"I must," Vlad protested. "Mr. Ferriday will be expecting me."

"It's too dangerous," she said. "The Untainted will be looking for trouble. They are always worse at night."

"A fact that has failed to deter you from sneaking about in the dark," said Vlad. When Dana did not reply, he continued. "I will not be long. Here," he pulled a folded piece of paper from his pocket, "will you keep this for me? It is important to me, so you can be assured that I will return for it."

"What is it?" she questioned as she unfolded the old manila paper.

"A poem," said Vlad. "It's about a sunset," he explained, stepping through the door. "I will tell you about it when I return."

CHAPTER TWENTY-ONE

THERE WERE NO STARS in the sky that night. A faint glow hung on the far side of the mountains, but only the quivering light, behind the town windows, was bright enough to cast shadows from the silhouettes of those intent on keeping the streets alive into the night.

By the time the last light of town had faded into the trees behind Vlad, even the mountains had vanished into the black wake left by the absent sun. The road and everything around him was lost, leaving only a view to regret at the realization that he might have asked Abbott for a lantern.

He brought his horse to a halt and waited a moment to allow her eyes to adjust to the new darkness. When he began again, he let go of the reins to allow the horse to follow whatever road there might be to Zander's Ferry. As his eyes were of little use, he closed them and listened to the creaking leather of the saddle. Allowing himself to sway with the rhythm of the horse's gait, the cadence lulled him into a state of repose.

It no longer mattered whether his eyes were open or closed, nor did it matter where he was going. Time itself had long since faded with the light, and his thoughts reverberated in a timeless echo contemplating the eternity of every step, until his thoughts became nothing more than the rise and fall of his chest, and he no longer remembered where it was he was going.

Somewhere in the eternal darkness, there came a flicker of something out of step, a desire to see something, if even for a little while. He looked hard into the darkness and his desire grew with the intensity of a light in the distance. "Zander's Ferry," he reminded himself.

When he had come to the point where the trees began to shake free of the darkness, he brought his horse to a halt, and led her into the treeline. He left the horse, while he reacquainted himself with the temporal world, and explored the small bit of earth floating in the void of eternity. In the center of the dark oasis stood a cabin beside the river.

He couldn't be sure of how long it had taken him to locate the door, though standing in front of it, he decided to give a knock. The door was opened enough to allow a man's face to squeeze through, searching for an answer for the disturbance.

"Good evening," said Vlad, "I was told I could find Ben Ferriday here."

"Who told you that?" asked the face.

"Ben Ferriday," he replied, his voice dropping.

"And who are you?" he was questioned further.

"Vlad," he answered.

At this the door slammed shut. Vlad stood watching his breath, and before he had decided whether or not to try knocking again, the door swung open and he was ushered inside, where he was met by another face, a familiar one. Ben Ferriday had his revolver trained on Vlad, and after the light from the fireplace had introduced the guest, he lowered his weapon and returned to his seat at a small log table.

"Sorry about that," said Ben. "Have a seat. Have you had supper? Zander cooked some fish. Oh," he assumed an air of formality, "Vlad, this is Zander. Zander, Vlad."

"Pleasure," said Vlad.

Zander sat down as though unaware of anyone else in his cabin. He was a large man with a round bushy beard. His hair was thick and matted, appearing as if he had recently cut it himself. The rough and plump features of his face made it difficult for Vlad to guess his age, though he assumed he must be in his thirties.

"Would you mind if I had a look at that revolver you are carrying?" Ben asked Vlad.

Vlad appeared visibly distressed by the request. There was a moment when he considered denying Ben's request, as he had the stagecoach conductor's on the Great Plains, but just as an ensuing charge of curiosity was about to overrun his discretion, Ben spoke again.

"Here," said Ben, setting a revolver on the table. "It's the same as this one, isn't it?"

Vlad looked with renewed curiosity to confirm the answer. It was the same as his revolver, with the exception of the engraving. He reached inside his coat to retrieve his revolver and set it on the table next to Ben's, and it was not until Ben reached for Vlad's gun that Vlad began to contemplate his decision.

Lifting Vlad's revolver, Ben turned the weapon over in his hands, as though turning back time. His look suggested he had left the table for somewhere neither Vlad nor Zander could follow. "How did you come by it?" he asked, finally, his eyes still polishing the cold metal.

"It was given to me by a friend," replied Vlad, "as a parting gift, when I left New York."

"It would be quite an extraordinary coincidence if your friend managed to acquire your father's revolver by chance after all these years," Ben asserted. "Who knows where it has been. I can only imagine where you have been. Victor had two children. If you are his boy, then you must have an older sister." Ben looked to Vlad, who remained silent for a time.

"Then Victor was my father," mumbled Vlad, finally.

"You don't resemble him," insisted Ben. "I can't compare you to your mother, as I never knew her. It was her death that brought your father and me

together. It was a turning point in my life." Ben looked
down at the table. "I was employed by Noah Haggerty
at the time," he continued. "For some reason, I felt
some empathy for Victor at the news of his loss. I
learned of it only after I had made off with some of his
livestock." He glanced up at Vlad, with a childlike look
of shame. "I felt terrible for what I had done, so much
so that I held back the livestock's value in silver and
told Noah I had lost some of the herd that I had
rustled. I took the money to your father, and we
became friends after that. I had to keep our friendship
a secret from Noah, or it would have meant trouble for
me and your father. It wasn't until later that I told
Victor what I had done, along with the true motivation
for bringing him the money that day, but he never held
it against me." There was another pause, and Ben
looked back to the table. "He couldn't let go of his wife.
He kept a necklace of hers with an engraving on it, like
this one," he held up the gun to show the engraving to
Vlad, and then to Zander in what appeared an
afterthought. "I had this revolver engraved, and I gave
it to your father" he said, handing the gun back to
Vlad. "It was quite a weapon in its time, and
apparently it is still making a name for itself," he said,
turning to Vlad. "I keep mine for sentimental reasons.
Is it true that you killed Fast Freddy Mangan?"

"It was not my intention," Vlad confessed hastily.
He was not ready to leave the subject of Victor

Marshak. "What can you tell me about my father?" he asked.

"What do you want to know?" said Ben, seeming to answer in passing.

"Everything," said Vlad.

"Everything," Ben repeated, with a smile. "Well, I don't know everything. I'll tell you what I remember, but first let me ask you, were you unaware of the bounty on Freddy Mangan's head?"

"I am not a bounty hunter," replied Vlad, in a more serious tone, and turned away, desiring to speak no more about Freddy Mangan or the bounty on his head. He watched the flames dancing in the fireplace, and noted the black residue that tarnished the stone walls of the firebox. It was far from the elegant structure that adorned Felicity's parlor. Zander had most likely constructed it himself, he thought. "If you did not kill Victor Marshak, then who did?" asked Vlad, turning back to Ben.

"Noah Haggerty's men," stated Ben as a matter-of-fact.

"And you did nothing?" pressed Vlad, reminded of his own attempt to save his friend Shimazu Gensai.

"I learned of it after the fact," exclaimed Ben. "I thought I had done well to hide my friendship with Victor. I stayed long enough to see Victor's body for myself, but the fact that Noah and the others had conspired without me was enough to convince me that I shouldn't stay longer."

Vlad saw no use in pressing Ben further. "Noah told me there was a belief in Iowa that this revolver was cursed," he said, in an inquiring tone.

"It's true," Ben affirmed. "I'm sure that is why they came for Victor during the night. They were afraid after what he had done to the Indians who raided his property. They tried to make it look like it was the Indians that came back for him, and that is the story that everyone seemed to accept, but Indians wouldn't have spared you and your sister, even though you were just babies."

Ben let his argument trail off and then returned to his dinner. He sat back in his chair with a piece of bread and began picking at it as though he were attempting to buy some time. Zander rose from his seat to place another log on the fire.

"If you've been talking to Noah," Ben spoke, at last, "then I suppose he told you that I killed Victor?"

"No," answered Vlad. "It was a man named Zach at the—"

"That son-of-a-bitch dared to—" Ben interrupted, slamming his fist on the table, "he's one of the men that was there the night they killed Victor."

"Why would Noah cause trouble for his debtors?" inquired Vlad. "Murder them even? It doesn't seem to make any sense."

"It does if you understand the nature of his business," stated Ben. "See, he lays claim to uncultivated lands, and then finances the sale of them to the less fortunate, who toil away, working them, trying to make a living off them, while paying back their debt to Noah. What they don't know is that their debt will never be forgiven, because Noah doesn't want the debt to be paid in full, he wants them to default, once the land has been made profitable. Eventually, the debtors will walk away from the land, once they've had enough harassment from Noah's men, or they turn up dead, like Victor. That way, on top of the money his debtors have paid, the land comes back to Noah worth far more than when he first laid claim to it. Only then will he part with it, provided someone is willing to pay a premium."

"Why kill my father?" asked Vlad. "Was he close to settling his debt?"

"No," Ben explained, "but he knew what was going on, and he began threatening Noah's men."

"Now, Noah is here in the Kansas territory trying to stay ahead of the frontier," suggested Vlad.

"That's about it," affirmed Ben. "I walked right by his land office today. Knowing Noah, he's likely to have something to do with the gang that fellow was blathering about earlier."

"The Untainted?" asked Zander. Both Ben and Vlad glanced over as if they'd forgotten he was still there. "That's Sheriff Healy's gang."

"Bart Healy?" asked Ben.

"That's right," answered Zander.

"Bart Healy was another of the old Iowa gang that worked for Noah," huffed Ben.

The end of Ben's remark was trampled by the sound of hooves charging past the cabin. Vlad and Ben stood to watch Zander slip out of the door. As soon as the door closed behind him, Vlad heard a voice shouting in the distance. "Go back inside and mind your business, Zander," came the voice. "And don't bother pulling the ferry back over. We'll be back through later."

Zander didn't open the door as Vlad would have expected, following the directions given by the voice. He began to worry for Zander the longer the door remained closed, until, finally, Zander slipped back inside, visibly upset. "You had to go talking about them," he started, as if Ben's evocation of Noah's name had summoned The Untainted. "Those bastards never pay the toll. They act like they own the whole damn countryside and everything in it. I think they're headed to make trouble for Bob Sobol."

"Dana's father?" Vlad spoke aloud. "Why do you think that?" he asked, his voice conveying concern.

"I heard one of them say that Bob was going to answer for his daughter," explained Zander, "and another of them suggested that they burn his barn down, again. Bob's in debt to Noah Haggerty, like half the other farmers around here. You might be right about those bastards," he said, turning to Ben. "They must be working for Haggerty. Maybe you need to shoot another one of them," he said, addressing Vlad once more. "Hell, shoot all of 'em. They're sitting ducks out there on the river. Just have to aim for the light," he finished, with a grin.

CHAPTER TWENTY-TWO

THE REMNANTS OF A FAMILIAR DREAM left Vlad with a foreboding anticipation. His recollection of Zander's mischievous grin faded with the evening light. He was back in his room at Felicity, and a damp cloth on his forehead offered the only hint as to how he had managed to pass the day in his bed.

The sight of Bella made him wonder how long he'd been dreaming. She sat beside the bed as she had the night he first arrived.

"Hello," she said.

Was it déjà vu? Was it still the first night, and his entire life at Felicity a dream? Was her name even Bella? Her dress seemed different than he remembered. Her cheek was red where she had been resting it in her hand.

"Vlad?" she tried again for a response.

"I don't remember coming back," mumbled Vlad. "How did I get here?" he asked, looking to Bella for assistance.

"A Mr. Ferriday brought you back," answered Bella. "You should rest."

"Where's Dana?" asked Vlad.

"No one knows," answered Bella.

"No one knows," repeated Vlad, in a questioning tone. He sat up and placed his feet on the wood floor. "Where is my bag?"

"It's here," said Bella, pointing. "I'll get you some water."

"Thank you," Vlad replied, reaching for his shoes, "but I can manage."

Outside his door, a girl whose name Vlad remembered as Mabel was following another of the girls down the hall toward him. Each greeted him as they rounded the stair railing. Mabel timidly asked where he had been, and he opened his mouth to answer, but found the question more difficult than he had expected. In the end he decided the simplest answer was that he had been in his room. Bella stepped in front of him, and he joined the train of girls heading down the stairs.

The hour's usual bustle was missing from the parlor below, but a loud commotion rose suddenly as Dana appeared and began running up the stairs. The madame was close behind, scolding Dana for the worry she had caused. The excitement ceased as Dana caught sight of Vlad, and the two stood staring at one another in the awkward silence. Before Vlad could question her, Dana turned and worked her way back down the stairs.

At the bottom of the stairs, the doorway to the parlor was blocked by the rest of Felicity's girls, who had gathered to watch the madame move to greet two men at the front door. After she commented on the fortunate timing of their arrival, she escorted them to the fireplace, and as the girls filed into the parlor after them, Vlad recognized the men as Abbott and Hugo Dunning, the magician from the party.

At the sight of Vlad, Abbott greeted him with surprise and the rest of the parlor turned to observe him with curiosity. Vlad, feeling whimsical, gave a bow, which brought giggles from among the girls and a smile to Abbott's face.

"Where is everyone tonight?" asked Vlad.

"He's been in his room," explained Mabel.

"We're under curfew," offered one of the other girls. "On account of what happened last night. Sheriff Healy is trying to catch the Devil."

Only Liz snickered. From the corner of his eye, Vlad saw Dana staring at him, but his eyes lost sight of the room about him, and he stood staring blankly at the floor.

"What happened last night?" another girl asked suddenly.

Vlad looked up to see Liz rolling her eyes.

"No one knows for sure," answered the madame. "That's why Abbott has brought Mr. Dunning, I presume."

"Always a pleasure to entertain, Madame," replied Hugo Dunning, and then motioned to everyone. "Please, sit down."

While everyone crowded around the fireplace, Abbott whispered something to Mr. Dunning. Once his audience had filled the seating by the fire and huddled together on the carpet, Mr. Dunning began. "Before I begin," he said, "I would like to point out to Miss Dana Sobol that, while the events of the story, which I am about to tell, took place at your father's farm, I can assure you that her family is quite alright."

Dana looked intently at Mr. Dunning and then turned again to study Vlad. Vlad tried not to make eye contact. When she glanced back at Mr. Dunning, he offered her a smile and then continued. "Now then, picture a night so dark you can't even see your hand in front of your face. The Untainted were out at Bob Sobol's. Terence Allen and Archie Winkler were rounding Bob's barn when they heard someone screaming on the other side. Terence pulled his rifle from the scabbard across the front of his saddle, and took off around the barn. Archie followed with a lantern in one hand and his revolver in the other. They heard a gunshot and abruptly the screaming stopped. When he reached the front of the barn, Archie held up the lantern, and what do you suppose he saw?"

"The Devil," shouted one of the girls.

Again, from the corner of his eye, Vlad could see Dana staring at him.

"That's right," continued Mr. Dunning. "There in the low light of Archie's lantern stood the Devil himself, looking at them with black hollow eyes. His face was bright red, and his eyes, mouth and nostrils were frozen open like the black pits of death's eternal abyss. It was as though he were screaming without making a sound, or the opposite of a scream, sucking the life from the world. He held his arms out to his sides like a bird. Midway, his right arm became a long blade coated with fresh blood. Next to the Devil stood the headless body of Marc Johnson—"

One of the girls made a muffled sound and sprung up from the floor. A few of the girls snickered, and everyone watched as she hurried from the room, disappearing into the hall. Vlad glanced briefly at Dana, who was eyeing him with suspicion.

Once everyone had turned back to Mr. Dunning, he began again. "Now, having his rifle already in hand, Terence took aim, but the Devil disappeared behind the body of Marc Johnson. Terence fired at Marc's body, but to no avail. Archie spurred his horse in a panic and took off toward the house. Terence called after him to return with the light, but Archie didn't so much as look back. Bob Sobol was on his porch when Archie came charging up and fell off his horse, pleading hysterically for Bob to let him in the house.

Bob took a lantern to the barn and found the dead bodies of Terence Allen, Marc Johnson, and Hank Evans."

"What happened to Hank Evans?" asked one of the girls.

"His body was lying not far from Marc's," answered Mr. Dunning. "There was a hole in his torso, where he'd been run clean through with a blade."

"So it was a man?" questioned Liz.

"Pardon?" returned Mr. Dunning.

"The Devil was a man," declared Liz, as a matter of fact. "Why would the Devil be afraid of a gun? Whoever it was used Marc's body as a shield."

"So it would seem," answered Mr. Dunning. "However, the only man I can think of who's proven himself daring enough to take such a fight to The Untainted, is sitting right there." said Mr. Dunning, gesturing to Vlad, "and he appears to have barely enough strength to stand."

Everyone turned to Vlad, who sat scratching his nose.

"Where were you last night?" Mr. Dunning questioned Vlad.

"Zander's Ferry," answered Vlad.

"Zander's Ferry is on the way to Bob Sobol's," remarked Mr. Dunning. "Is it not?"

"If it were me," said Vlad, with a half grin, "I would have chosen to disguise myself as something more frightening than the Devil."

"What could be more frightening than the Devil?" asked Bella.

"A priest," replied Vlad.

Everyone laughed, except for Bella.

"You're making fun of me," Bella protested.

"No I'm not," Vlad assured her. "What a metaphor for death. A priest is a walking reminder of it, he dies every day for the sake of his virtue, and he wears only black to remind himself of the life he has given up. Think about it. On any given night, who would you rather walk into the parlor, the Devil or a priest? As long as the Devil had not come for you, you might go so far as to offer him a drink." He continued over the sound of laughter. "However, if a priest were to walk into the parlor, regardless of whom he had come to visit, I would expect everyone in the house to sneak out the back door." This time, he conceded to the laughter.

"I think this town would believe a sighting of the Devil over a sighting of a priest," quipped Liz.

"I saw a priest just the other day," returned Vlad, fueling the laughter, "walking up the street toward Felicity. I'm being serious." His voice was lost to the chatter that surged among the rest of the company.

"He really believes he saw a priest," declared Liz after examining Vlad. The room settled down as she continued, "Archie Winkler saw the Devil, and now Vlad's seeing ghosts."

"Do you believe in ghosts?" asked Bella, after Vlad did not respond.

"No," answered Vlad.

"I do," Dana interjected. "When we were passing through Missouri on our way here, my father and I saw a little girl walking alongside the road. When we came upon her she darted into the road and passed right through our wagon. We stopped to search for her, but she had vanished. Once we entered town, my father mentioned what we had seen, and everyone there referred to the girl by name. They said she had died after falling into a well a few years prior. Apparently, many travelers had reported seeing her walking the road to town." When Dana finished her story, she turned to Vlad as though awaiting a response.

"That is a rather convincing account," said Vlad, forcing his words as he pulled a handkerchief from his pocket. He quickly bloodied the handkerchief in a fit of violent coughing. The light in the room grew dim and darkness took hold, quickly closing in around him. A faint light from the fireplace persisted for a moment, like the sun, or a lone star, caught in the last glimpse of consciousness,   then   everything   went   black.

CHAPTER TWENTY-THREE

IN A WEAKENED STATE, Vlad lay still, attempting to draw in the transcendent beauty of the eyes that watched over him, brightened by the reflection of a candle flame that burned steadily at the head of his bed. Propped upon her elbow, Dana's head rested in her hand as she looked down at him. Her other hand was on his chest. The soft mattress of his bed settled beneath them, pressing them close to share their warmth beneath the covers.

She appeared to be staring at his chest, which made Vlad increasingly anxious about the tiny red moles scattered across his pale skin. "These red spots on your chest," said Dana, at last, "they resemble constellations of the stars." She paused again to examine him, and he decided he didn't mind showing off a map of the stars on his chest. He recalled Molly's suggestion that his countenance was the envy of higher society, the pale beauty of a cursed youth.

"I had the most wonderful dream," whispered Vlad. It seemed speaking deepened his breaths. "The priest I saw," he continued, "he was standing on Longs Peak, pulling the sun into the sky with a rope. You and I were watching from the roof of Felicity, and then you kissed me. I felt so light, and I couldn't fight the urge, so I jumped from the roof. I glided toward the ground, though I did not touch it. Instead, I glided down the street and then up over the houses. I kept rising higher until I was looking down at the mountains."

Dana leaned over and kissed him, as though a conjectured re-enactment from his dream. "That sounds like a wonderful dream," she said, sitting up.

"Is Hugo Dunning still here?" asked Vlad, attempting to verify his sense of time and set the stage for an apology.

Yes," answered Dana, "he is with Liz."

"I am sorry you were left to learn of yesterday's events from a storyteller," said Vlad.

"I suppose you were making another impression, last night," said Dana.

Vlad smiled, and his laugh quickly became a cough.

"Thank you," said Dana.

"I suppose," said Vlad, catching his breath, "it was fortunate that I chanced going to Zander's Ferry. I should tell you, it is Noah Haggerty whom the sheriff and The Untainted answer to. It is Noah who enslaved my father with impossible debt, and he has done the same to your father. He uses The Untainted to ensure the debt is never repaid."

"After our encounter with Mr. Ferriday," replied Dana, "I became suspicious of Noah Haggerty. I went to his house to see if he was there. He has just returned from Salt Lake City. After everything that has happened, I don't know what he'll do. He has threatened to have Felicity burned more than once. I suspect my being here is enough of a provocation."

"I will not allow any harm to come to you, or Felicity," said Vlad.

"Nor will I," said Dana. "I'm going to kill him."

"What?" said Vlad. His attempt to sit worsened his coughing.

"Lie still," said Dana, placing her hand back on his chest. "He is responsible for the death of my brother, as is the sheriff, and I will have my revenge, tonight."

Vlad placed his hand on top of Dana's. "My sister," he forced the words, "my father, they are both dead because of Noah Haggerty. I will do it."

"You can't even get out of bed," argued Dana. "I have to do it, for my brother."

"Wait," said Vlad. "I will be fine by morning. Stay with me. Please."

Dana stared at Vlad for a moment, then lay back down beside him. They lay still for a time, before Vlad broke the silence.

"Abbott mentioned that the madame is helping your father," remarked Vlad.

"Yes," said Dana, "in return for my love, but it is not something I can give her. She is like a mother to me, but a mother should not want a daughter for her body.

My father's debt will be settled when Noah Haggerty is dead."

At Dana's words, Vlad realized that he was afraid. Perhaps it was an appeal to adventure, but he felt it was more a sense of duty. He feared the night would not return his strength and he would be unable to fight for his friends. He had come too far to die with regret. "Do you have my poem?" he asked Dana.

"It is there," she assured him, "on the table. It is beautiful."

"Would you like to have it," he asked her.

"Yes," replied Dana, "but–"

"It would be an honor to me, if you were to keep it," said Vlad. "When I was on the Great Plains, I met a man who spoke to the Indians there. According to him, the Indians believe that when we die we become stars in the sky. Unless one dies a cowardly death, that is. In that case, one would be taken to a village of spirits in the south." Vlad paused to clear his throat, then continued. "This man asked me where I would go when I die. I told him I would go to the village of spirits. He seemed quite taken aback by my answer. He seemed puzzled, and I can understand why he might have thought it puzzling. One might expect both the brave and the cowardly to answer the same for that question, but I did not choose as I did because I thought myself a coward. I chose the village in the south, not for its proximity, but for the spirits. A village is where people go to live, and I want to live."

Dana kept her hand on Vlad's chest and leaned over to kiss his forehead. "I think I understand why you answered as you did."

Vlad lay still in a daze, staring at the ceiling. After a moment, he turned to Dana in a delayed reaction to her affection and returned a smile. "I've been thinking about my answer," he continued. "I think if I were asked the question again, I would answer differently. When I have left this world and am no longer aware of the living, what does it matter to me if I become a star, or a shadow? If those who knew me wish to see me in the reflection of someone else or in the twinkling of the night sky, why would I care to take that from them? I certainly don't want to live forever, no matter the village in which I might reside."

"There's something about you," said Dana.

"I'm nice," said Vlad, smiling, and attempting to turn his cough into laughter.

"Yes," said Dana, "but that's not it. There's something else about you."

"Do not say innocence," replied Vlad.

"Why?" asked Dana. "Have you been told this before?"

"How could you say that," said Vlad, coughing, "having seen the things I've done."

"You didn't do it for yourself," said Dana. "I wish I was more like you."

Again, Vlad tried to turn his coughing to laughter. His breaths shortened, and the light in the room began to grow dim, as before. A small flicker persisted for a moment, like a candle flame, or the faint light of the fireplace in the parlor. The soft light warmed him with the hope that his strength would soon return.

CHAPTER TWENTY-FOUR

THE LIGHT STAYED with Vlad until morning, and he opened his eyes to find it pouring through his window. He lay in his bed, focused on the ceiling, and just as he was beginning to wonder how long he had been staring vaguely without a thought to consider, he heard a great commotion outside in the hall.

Dana was gone, though the weight of her hand on his chest seemed to remain. It was heavier now, so much so that it was difficult for him to breathe. He smelled smoke, and struggled to get out of bed, noting that his strength had not returned.

He managed to dress himself, but was unable to find his revolver. Feeling dizzy, he knelt down and crawled to the foot of his bed. His bag was gone. A sudden realization filled him with a sense of urgency. Using the bed to pull himself up, he stumbled to the door. Looking back to the table by the bed, He noticed that his poem was gone.

The house was in disarray. He pushed his way down the stairs past walking mounds of lingerie. In the parlor, two girls were peeking through curtains by the front door. Others were rushing down the stairs laden with whatever belongings they could carry. The parlor furniture was covered in piles of dresses and corsets. The sounds of crying and shuffling feet reverberated through the upstairs floorboards. At the sight of the madame stepping out of her office, one of the girls by the front door rushed over to plead for help. The madame brushed the girl's hair with her fingers and stepped around her en route to relieve her from her watch at the front door.

Leaning against the bar, Vlad worked his way toward the door. As he neared the madame, she turned back to the parlor. When she spotted him, she stared as though he were a ghost, the apparition of something lost that might ease her pain.

"I thought you were dead," she exclaimed.

Vlad was unsure how to respond. Had he managed to wake from the eternal sleep? He could not be far removed. If he let go, he would surely fall back into oblivion.

"Where is Dana?" asked the madame.

Vlad had seen the look in her eyes before. It was the same look he had seen in the eyes of the man draped over his wife in the stagecoach, a panicked look, a silent plea for help.

"What is going on?" asked Vlad, attempting to force his weakened voice over the commotion.

"The fire is spreading," answered the madame. Her eyes darted about as though she were expecting the parlor to burst into flames.

"What fire?" asked Vlad.

"The land office burned down last night," she said, looking at Vlad as if to ascertain his comprehension. "Noah Haggerty's house was also burned ... with him in it." At these words, the madame's eyes appeared to gloss over as though she might begin to cry, but she continued. "The sheriff was found stabbed to death in his bed. Supposedly, Gene Ballard found him after he saw the goddam Devil leaving the sheriff's house. What have you done?"

"I tried to prevent this," Vlad assured her. "Dana was gone when I woke." He was consoled by the fact that Dana's whereabouts were unknown.

The madame started toward the hallway, but stopped and turned back to Vlad. Her hand trembled as she brushed a loose strand of hair behind her ear. "Zach Gibson and Archie Winkler were found gunned down in front of the Northern Exchange," she said, as her eyes darted about more erratically than before. She dropped her arm and wandered into the hall, dragging her feet as though she were no longer in control of them. The madame's wits seemed to have been split down the middle and drawn back like curtains, leaving her dangling as a puppet, animated by some volition other than her own. Vlad pressed on, in the opposite direction, toward the front door.

Outside, the ground was white, and a light snow blurred the crisp contrasting lines of dark wood buildings that appeared suspended in the enveloping incandescence. Pillars of black smoke rose above the rooftops and disappeared into the grey sky.

Still dizzy, he looked around for something to take hold of, though nothing but soft white lay about him. Even his shadow had left him. Perhaps Dana had taken it as well. He smiled as he fell to his knees in the street and pressed his hands into the snow. His fingers were blue, and as he looked at them he felt his mind slipping as it would before surrendering to sleep. His body jolted as though he'd been startled from a dream, and a terrible anxiety remained. His heart pounded in his ears as if to drown out the one thought he had prepared for this moment. Struggling to breathe, he laughed at the pain in his chest, pain that spurred emotion intimately entangled in a greater measure of emotions, defined as any measurement must be, by a beginning and an end. "It is worth it," he said, remembering the thought. His heart caught fire as he felt a spark ignite somewhere in the quiet cosmos beyond the incandescent haze, a new star made bright by the encircling darkness.

More books from
Harvard Square Editions:

People and Peppers, Kelvin Christopher James

Gates of Eden, Charles Degelman

Love's Affliction, Fidelis Mkparu

Transoceanic Lights, S. Li

Close, Erika Raskin

Anomie, Jeff Lockwood

Living Treasures, Yang Huang

Nature's Confession, J.L. Morin

Love and Famine, Han-ping Chin

Dark Lady of Hollywood, Diane Haithman

How Fast Can You Run, Harriet Levin Millan

Appointment with ISIL, Joe Giordano

Never Summer, Tim Blaine

Parallel, Sharon Erby